NO ORDINARY THING

G. Z. SCHMIDT

HOLIDAY HOUSE · NEW YORK

Printed and bound in August 2020 at Maple Press, York, PA, USA.

www.holidayhouse.com

First Edition

10 9 8 7 6 5 4 3 2 1

Library of Congress Cataloging-in-Publication Data

Names: Schmidt, G. Z. (Gail Zhuang), author.
Title: No ordinary thing / by G. Z. Schmidt.
Description: First edition. | New York : Holiday House, [2020] |
    Audience: Ages 8-12. | Audience: Grades 4-6. | Summary: A
    mysterious stranger brings to shy, orphaned, twelve-year-old
    Adam a magical snow globe that sends him on adventures through
    time, and then returns him to his uncle's New York City bakery.
Identifiers: LCCN 2019055030 | ISBN 9780823444229 (hardcover)
Subjects: CYAC: Time travel—Fiction. | Magic—Fiction. |
    Snowdomes—Fiction. | Orphans—Fiction.
Classification: LCC PZ7.1.S33618 No 2020 | DDC [Fic]—dc23
LC record available at https://lccn.loc.gov/2019055030

For Emily, my first reader

CONTENTS

CHAPTER ONE

NEW YORK CITY, 1999

About two hours before midnight on a busy street in Manhattan, a man in a raincoat appeared out of nowhere. His sudden presence should have been startling, but no one took notice of him. That particular part of New York bustled with cars and people at all hours, so much so that nobody really saw each other in the crowds. Everyone had other business to attend to, and a stranger lingering in the shadows—even one who had quite literally materialized from thin air—did not capture their interest that October evening.

The man in the raincoat walked several blocks until the path broke off to reveal a cobblestone side street leading to a quieter patch of neighborhood. He stood at its edge and silently observed the area with a smile.

If anyone *had* bothered to take a glance at him that night, they might've found it slightly odd that the man's

raincoat was dripping wet when it hadn't rained anywhere nearby that day.

They might've found it odder still that he carried
what looked like a snow globe in his hands, with the care
of someone cradling a cherished pet.

But New York City was full of oddballs, so again, no
one bothered with him.

Which is unfortunate, because had these passersby
stopped to ask who he was and what he was doing there,
they would've found the answer the oddest of all.

Because our friend in the raincoat wasn't supposed
to exist yet.

CHAPTER TWO

THE VISITOR IN THE RAINCOAT

The same cobblestone street had a tiny bakery on the corner called the Biscuit Basket.

Ask anyone in the neighborhood, and they would tell you the Biscuit Basket was a "perfectly adequate bakery, now please get out of my way"—which was a sore understatement, because the bakery's goods were far above average.

In the early mornings, when the sun had barely tinted the glassy skyscrapers along the East River, the aroma of freshly baked breads and chocolate croissants wafted from the tiny brick building and filled every inch of the street.

Despite its enticing smells and first-rate offerings, however, the bakery had only a scarcely adequate share of customers. On good days, mornings saw one or two adults who stopped by for a quick sugar doughnut before work. In the afternoons came the neighborhood kids fresh

3

from school, their pockets jingling with allowance money as they gathered around the colorful array of cupcakes along the counter. And of course there were the occasional weary ladies in large, fancy hats who needed two orders of peach cobbler, immediately if you please, for their evening book club every third Tuesday of the month.

But on bad days, the Biscuit Basket had hardly any visitors at all. On those days, the baker—a stocky and balding man named Henry—could be seen waiting behind the counter anxiously, or else rearranging the cakes at the display window for the thousandth time, or else trying to attract customers by offering free samples of strawberry-and-almond tarts to passersby.

It wasn't Henry's fault. No matter how hard he pounded the dough, no matter how fast he mixed the cream and sugar, the Biscuit Basket never seemed to entice quite enough customers to its corner of the street. Not when an enormous candy shop, a coffee shop, and two other bakeries sat just two streets over.

So on those lonely days, Henry would look wistfully at the untouched pastries that had grown stale and hope he had enough money to pay the rent.

It was such a day on that Saturday evening when our story begins. A few hours before the mysterious man in the raincoat appeared, the streets were cold and dreary and darkening with October gloom. Not a single customer had stopped by the bakery, where Henry had sat behind the counter for the better part of the day.

Finally, it was closing time. Henry sighed and looked up from the dollar bills he was counting. Money had been tight that week as always, but at least this time he could afford to donate most of the leftovers instead of saving them for the next day's discount shelf. Baked goods are never as tasty the day after.

"Adam," the baker called to his nephew, "do you mind delivering the leftover breakfast pastries to the Hole?"

Henry had one helper in the shop—his twelve-year-old nephew, Adam. Adam was small for his age, with pale skin and eyes the color of charcoal. One could occasionally glimpse the top of the boy's tousled dark hair behind the kitchen window. Or, if you were to watch carefully, you might see him slip your order of lemon custard on the counter before disappearing to the back without a peep.

Because of his uncle's job, Adam spent his time either at school or at the bakery. Adam didn't mind. He didn't have too many friends. Adam was, by all accounts, a peculiar boy. But we shall get to that later.

"Sure, Uncle Henry," Adam answered. He closed the pages of *Self-Guide to Caring for Mice* he was reading and collected the unsold pastries from that day into a large paper bag. He lugged the bag outside.

The stars were hidden in the cloudy night sky, the moon barely visible. Adam cautiously made his way down the sidewalk, taking care to stay in the parts lit by streetlights as he approached the Hole.

Most things don't belong in holes. Holes are damp and dark, and ideal for dog bones, trash, and pesky night critters that dig up people's vegetable gardens. In the same way, the Hole was what most people called the local homeless shelter and, with it, the city's unwanted inhabitants.

As usual, the Hole's tired brick walls and murky windows greeted Adam. Several disheveled folks stood outside the scratched door, their worn faces half-hidden in the shadows, their hands stuffed in their pockets. None of them seemed to have smiled in a long time. Adam sometimes wondered if they'd forgotten how.

He passed them silently and went inside the battered building to the kitchen. A skinny, elderly man in a wheelchair sat stirring a large pot of what smelled like cabbage stew. Upon hearing Adam's footsteps, he turned his tanned and weathered face to the boy and broke into a nearly toothless grin.

"Hello, fellow!" said the old man.

"Hi, Victor. Special delivery," Adam murmured. He placed the bag of muffins and croissants in the man's outstretched hands. "Extras from today."

Victor was a resident of the homeless shelter. He spent his mornings on the streets, chatting with the other homeless folks or telling entertaining tales to children. He spent his evenings cooking for the hungry. Victor was one of the few people Adam didn't mind talking to. The old man never made fun of Adam for his eyes or size.

Victor gratefully took the pastries and held the bag close to his scruffy beard. "They smell wonderful," he sighed, and put the crinkled bag in the basket attached to his wheelchair. Rumor had it that he lost his leg in a street fight against a bulldog. Or was it an alligator? Victor changed the story every time he told it.

Adam mumbled something in reply. Victor leaned forward with his ear cupped. "Sorry, sonny, my hearing isn't as good as it once was."

The twelve-year-old said louder, "There's a blueberry muffin in there. Your favorite."

"Excellent. I'll make sure to save that for myself. Did you know, just this morning, I met a lady who grows blueberries for a living? Right in a little garden on the roof of her apartment building. Just imagine the mathematical probability of a blueberry patch's existence on a rooftop like that . . ."

Normally, Adam would stay longer to listen to Victor recount his day's adventures and conversations. The old man had a way of telling stories that instantly captivated listeners, even if the story was about something as simple as going to the grocery store for milk.

But that evening, something particular was weighing on Adam's mind, and he itched to return home as soon as possible.

Victor seemed to read his thoughts. "How is Speedy?" the old man asked.

Speedy was Adam's pet mouse, rescued from the

confines of the Biscuit Basket's kitchen cabinet one fateful evening two months ago. Uncle Henry had been preparing a batch of vanilla cupcakes and was searching the cabinet for a box of rainbow sprinkles when the white mouse peeked out from behind a jar of flour. Before Uncle Henry could react, the mouse had zoomed down the baker's outstretched arm onto the counter. Uncle Henry, who liked rodents as much as he liked moldy cupcakes, didn't hesitate to grab his bread knife. It was Adam's dismayed "Wait, don't hurt it!" that stopped what would have been a disastrous evening for Speedy.

Speedy was a big reason Adam didn't need friends at school. The mouse did what any boy could do: eat, run, sleep, listen. What's more, Speedy could do tricks. He could climb onto Adam's hand when his name was called, and wiggle his pink nose and soft whiskers against Adam's fingers. He could stand up on his tiny hind legs when directed. He had once even crawled across a pencil Adam held in midair. Adam was very fond of the dear mouse, though he wisely avoided letting Uncle Henry know he'd adopted it.

"Speedy's fine." Adam avoided Victor's eyes and cleared the catch in his throat. "I have to get back home. See you later."

"Goodbye! Say hello to your uncle for me."

Adam and his uncle lived in the small apartment above the Biscuit Basket. It had one bedroom the size of a normal closet, a narrow kitchen, a tight bathroom, and a living room that might have been spacious had it not doubled as Uncle Henry's bedroom and a storage space for baking utensils. The one good thing about a cramped apartment above a bakery was that every nook and cranny smelled of baked goods.

After returning home, Adam raced to his bedroom. He stepped over the animal care brochures and half-finished library books he'd borrowed, and reached under his narrow mattress to retrieve the old shoebox where Speedy slept. He gently prodded the white mouse, but it didn't budge. The mouse hadn't moved in a day, and its breaths were faint.

"Come on, buddy," Adam whispered. "I brought you something." He placed a smashed blueberry inside the box next to Speedy. Blueberries, according to *Self-Guide to Caring for Mice*, had "antioxidants"—nutritious energy that supposedly boosted the body. It should make Speedy move again.

Adam waited, but nothing happened.

"Adam?" Uncle Henry peered inside the room.

Adam shoved the box behind him, but not before his uncle had caught a glimpse. His uncle sighed.

"Adam, we've talked about this," he said. "Mice are not household pets."

"I know . . ."

"They spoil the flour and ruin everything."

"Not Speedy. He only eats the lettuce and fruits I feed him."

Uncle Henry gave another sigh and shook his head.

Some people said the baker looked just like Adam's father. This made sense, since siblings tend to look alike, although from what Adam could remember, his father had been leaner and taller, with fair hair and tanner skin, whereas Uncle Henry stayed pale from a lack of sunlight due to working many hours indoors. Adam took after his mother more, who had dark hair like Adam and had also been short for her age.

Uncle Henry opened his mouth to say something—likely a lecture about how mice are the reason exterminators have secure jobs—but before he could launch into his spiel, the doorbell chimed downstairs. Adam and his uncle exchanged a puzzled look. The bakery was closed.

"It's probably the landlord," said Uncle Henry with a slightly worried expression.

Adam followed his uncle downstairs. Visits from the dreaded landlord, especially at night, were never a good sign. The last time the landlord had arrived, Uncle Henry had gotten a warning letter for being late on the rent.

It was not the landlord. Instead, a cheerful stranger in a raincoat stood outside the door, waving to Adam and his uncle through the glass. He held a map in one hand, and ran his other hand through his wet, graying wheat-colored hair.

"I'm terribly sorry, I know it's late," the man called through the door. "But I was passing by, and, well, may

I say your cakes look fabulous? I simply *must* buy one. Or five. I hope you're not closed?"

After the long, empty day of no customers, Uncle Henry was so giddy at the potential business that he threw open the door and practically kissed the stranger's hand. The stranger had barely finished introducing himself as J.C. Walsh before the baker started speaking a mile a minute about the goods available.

"We have every kind of cake imaginable," said Uncle Henry. "Carrot cake, coffee cake, a red velvet cake that I can frost for you right now with the most scrumptious whipped cream you've ever tasted . . ."

"Excellent," said the man in the raincoat. "I'll have that red velvet cake, please." Then he added, "Make it with *buttercream* frosting—my favorite—and I'll pay double what you'd normally charge."

This was more than Uncle Henry could bear. He stammered a "Y-yes, of c-course," and stumbled into the kitchen in a daze. There followed a clanging of pots and bowls, and the sound of Uncle Henry's humming was soon accompanied by the soothing whir of the mixer.

Adam was about to head back upstairs when, to his surprise, the man in the raincoat turned to address him.

"You must be Adam Lee Tripp."

Growing up in a city as large as New York had taught Adam not to share personal information with strangers. He didn't answer, but stared blankly at the man, who stared back with a big smile.

"It's been a while," said the stranger, his voice softening.

The man reached into his pocket and held up a snow globe. Inside the glass sphere was a miniature cityscape that looked just like Manhattan, sprinkled with bright snow confetti. The man gazed at the snow globe in a sort of admiration.

"The one in which past days unfold," he murmured. Then, as if he suddenly remembered Adam was there, he raised his head and said, "Speedy is sick and dying, but great things are in store for you."

Adam gaped at the man. He had no idea how the stranger knew about Speedy. *Could he be a fortune-teller?* Adam wondered. Uncle Henry always said that fortune-tellers were con artists wrapped in glitzy shawls who charged twenty dollars per reading, and whose predictions were most of the time as wrong as two left feet.

"Speedy's not dead yet," Adam said hoarsely, but he said it so quietly he doubted the man heard.

"Hear me, Adam?" the man persisted. "Great things await you. Fantastic things. You will find new friends in new places, and go on journeys more magical than you could have ever imagined."

From the kitchen in the back, Uncle Henry shouted, "Do you want fondant roses on the cake?"

"Yes, that would be delightful!" the man in the raincoat called back. He put the snow globe back in his pocket and winked at Adam. "Tonight, go up to the attic," he instructed with a mysterious smile. "Your adventures await you there."

Adam decided this character was not to be trusted. "Um, okay, sir," he said, taking a step back. "Bye."

He ran upstairs before the man could say another word. As soon as Adam was alone, he checked on Speedy again. The blueberry lay untouched. The mouse still didn't move.

Adam felt sick. His throat burning, he gently placed the cardboard box back under the bed. He then angrily kicked his copy of *Self-Guide to Caring for Mice* across the floor before crawling under the covers and turning off the lights.

He spent a long time thinking about the man in the raincoat. The stranger was a weirdo; he'd known it as soon as the man said Adam's name. And then the man mentioned the attic, of all places, which was by far Adam's least favorite room in the building.

It was a long time before he finally drifted uncomfortably to sleep.

Little did Adam know, the stranger was right. Things were about to change in ways he couldn't begin to imagine.

CHAPTER THREE

A TRIP TO THE ATTIC

Earlier I mentioned that Adam was a peculiar boy.

"Adam is a good student," wrote his sixth-grade teacher, Ms. Basil, on his first report card of the year, "but he never interacts with his peers."

The year before that, his fifth-grade teacher, Mr. Lemon, observed, "Adam sits by himself at recess and reads the entire time. Every single day."

And the year before that, Mrs. Rosemary, Adam's fourth-grade teacher, noted, "Adam has not spoken a single word this entire year in class, other than to mumble requests to use the restroom."

Ever since kindergarten, Adam had kept his distance from other kids. In the classroom, he'd always pick the farthest seat possible from everyone else. He sat by himself at lunchtime. At recess, whenever someone asked him to join in a game, be it hide-and-seek, hopscotch, or freeze tag, he would adamantly shake his head. He kept himself inside an invisible cocoon, the way a caterpillar hides from the outside world.

The thing about isolating yourself is that once you do it often enough, people tend to avoid you in return. Eventually, kids started making up nasty rumors about Adam. Nicknames, too. His belongings started vanishing and turning up in the bathroom toilets. In sixth grade, a few classmates had taken up the hobby of shoving him into the school lockers whenever they had the chance.

Unfortunately for them, Adam was as nimble as he was invisible, and he usually managed to stay out of the bullies' way.

The school counselor, Ms. Ginger, believed there was an easy solution to every problem. A fierce woman with fiery red hair, she frequently assessed Adam's shyness and did not hesitate to offer Uncle Henry her unyielding opinion.

"As a professionally licensed counselor, I recommend Adam join an after-school club so he can meet children with similar interests. I myself am an honorary member of the Amateur Actors Association. (We have our first musical this summer, by the way. I'll be playing the mermaid in the second act. Please remember to book tickets in advance.) Anyway, I know firsthand how wonderful after-school activities can be. Boy Scouts, for example, is a great way to build character. (Just ask my darling sons—did you know my eldest earned his second merit badge last month? Very proud of him.) Not to mention the splendid troop uniforms . . ."

But after-school activities meant spare time and money, neither of which Adam or his uncle had. So Adam did not wear a splendid uniform, but instead wore secondhand clothes from thrift stores. Uncle Henry owned neither a car nor a TV.

At least they never went hungry. Uncle Henry would make his own breads and pasta, since it was significantly cheaper than buying from the grocery store. They'd often finish leftover items from the bakery, soaking them in watery soup so the bread wouldn't taste stale.

Adam understood his uncle was poor, and tried to help out whenever he could. He was fine with not getting an allowance like the other kids. On his last birthday, he didn't complain when he received not a single present, much less the red seven-speed bicycle he'd been eyeing for months in the bike shop's window. He skipped the bookstores and borrowed books for free from the public library. The one downside to that was all the fill-in-the-blank adventure stories and crossword puzzles tended to be scribbled in already.

It helped that Uncle Henry was one of the best bakers around, even if not enough people seemed to know it. Adam may have had to ignore the dollar ice cream line in the school cafeteria, but he had plenty of delicious sweets to come home to.

No, despite his financial situation, despite avoiding

people in the school hallways, Adam was not a mean kid. You probably already guessed that when you learned how Adam spared Speedy's life in the kitchen.

Ultimately, however, he couldn't save the mouse.

Just like he couldn't save his parents.

The first instance of loss, while tragic, was not peculiar. Although Adam didn't know it, Speedy was already one and a half years old when rescued. And mice typically don't live longer than two years.

As for his parents' accident, there was no way Adam could have prevented that disaster. But we are getting ahead of ourselves.

About a week after the strange man in the raincoat visited the bakery, Uncle Henry broke the news to Adam: they were short on rent that month.

"There's old stuff in our attic that we don't need anymore," said his uncle, avoiding eye contact. "If you wouldn't mind picking out some things after breakfast, I can sell them to the pawn shop later . . ." He trailed off uncomfortably.

Adam nibbled the last bit of his toast and nodded, reluctantly. The tiny storage space was dusty, stuffy, and home to dozens of crawling spiders and other abominations with more than six legs. Adam wasn't afraid of bugs, but he hated when they appeared out of nowhere. He hated when anything appeared out of nowhere.

After breakfast, he climbed the ladder in their apartment that led to the attic. Forgotten boxes and broken suitcases lay scattered across the creaky floorboards. Adam made his way across the room, guided by a shaft of muted white sunlight that streamed through a small circular window. After half an hour of searching, he set aside several promising items that he suspected would sell for a decent amount of money—mostly things like candelabras, extra silverware, old curtains, and rusty tools.

Then, inevitably, one of the boxes in the corner caught his attention. The cardboard was worn, and the handwritten label on the box had faded. But one could still make out the familiar name: *Tripp*.

Adam's heart raced. That particular box was one he had gone through only a few times in his life—and for good reason. Today, though, he felt drawn to open it.

A stale cloud of dust greeted him as he carefully lifted the lid. His parents, international aid workers and avid travelers, had owned a large collection of paper maps and atlases. From what Adam knew, they'd been part of an explorers' club of some sort. Several of the maps and thick books sat in the box, nested among souvenirs from all over the world. Adam picked up a carved wooden seashell from when his parents had visited the shores of Brazil. Beneath that was a volcanic rock from Hawaii, the jagged piece of earth looking more like a black, deformed kitchen sponge. His parents had reportedly climbed an extinct volcano when they visited the tropical island. Snuggled against the rock was a smiling porcelain cat with Chinese symbols painted on its body, one of his mother's heirlooms from her birthplace.

He dug past a few more miscellaneous items, setting them on the floor beside him—keychains, plastic cups with faraway city names printed on them in shiny block letters, bead bracelets, an antique admission ticket to a carnival in New Jersey—until he found the faded postcard. His parents had sent it from Norway, just a few days before the accident. Like the box, the edges of the postcard were frayed, and the ink had smeared in some places, but Adam already knew the message by heart.

Dear Adam,
Hello from Norway! We hope all is well back
home. Uncle Henry left us a message at our hotel
to tell us you won second place in the kindergarten
egg-and-spoon-race derby! We're so proud of you.
We miss you and can't wait to be back next
Tuesday. Someday when you're older, we'll take
you on these trips with us. Soon you'll be as tired of
airplanes as we are! (Though they're certainly more
ordinary and predictable than other forms of travel,
shall we say?)
No matter where or when or how, we want to
do all the good we can in the world. It's such a big,
amazing place full of wonders. And you never know

which of these wonders are in store for you, or what
you might find!

Love,
Mom and Dad

Adam would never sell any of his parents' personal belongings, of course. But neither did he like to look at them for too long. He started to place the postcard back in the box. Then he did a double take.

Underneath the postcard, wedged next to an atlas, was a snow globe. Adam vaguely remembered seeing it displayed on the topmost shelf of his parents' bookcase in their old apartment.

The snow globe looked like an ordinary snow globe, the glass sphere a little bigger than a grapefruit, and glued onto a square wooden base. However, unlike most snow globes, the inside of the glass was clear and blank. It contained only a layer of confetti snow—nothing else. On the corner of the base was a small engraving of a compass rose.

Adam remembered the uncanny stranger in the raincoat who had shown up with his own snow globe a week ago. *Go up to the attic,* he had instructed Adam.

Nonsense, Adam fumed. *It doesn't mean anything. The man was a lunatic.*

He was bitter at himself for even thinking of the man in the raincoat, who had correctly guessed Speedy was about to die. Earlier that week, Uncle Henry had prepared an empty egg carton for Speedy's funeral. "A dead mouse can't feel the cold," his uncle had said in a failed attempt to comfort him.

They'd buried the mouse in the dumpster out back, since they didn't have a yard.

Adam placed the rest of his parents' keepsakes back inside the box. He gathered the tools, candelabra, and old curtains he'd found for Uncle Henry into a duffel bag, slung the strap over his shoulder, and started to climb back down the ladder.

But then, for some reason he couldn't explain, Adam stopped. He set down his bundle and went back to his parents' box.

The next time he made his way to the ladder, he had the snow globe with him.

Downstairs, the bakery was devoid of customers. Adam placed the bag of items from the attic on the counter, right above the untouched rows of breakfast pastries that were slowly going stale.

Uncle Henry was in the kitchen. "Did you find anything?" he called through the window, to which Adam held up the candelabra in reply.

His uncle came over with a batch of mouse-shaped

frosted sugar cookies. "Here, I made these for you. You've been glum all week."

Adam knew they were meant to cheer him up about Speedy. For his uncle's sake, he pretended to enjoy a piece of mouse tail, even though he didn't feel like eating anything. They chewed in silence. His uncle cleared the plates.

"All right, I'm heading out," said Uncle Henry. He hung the CLOSED sign on the bakery door, then picked up the bag of items Adam had gathered. "This is everything, right?"

"Wait!" Adam jumped up and removed the snow globe from the duffel. "Not this." He placed the snow globe on the counter.

After Uncle Henry left, Adam went back to his cramped bedroom. There wasn't a lot to do at home, especially now that he no longer spent his free time teaching Speedy new tricks. He sat for a while and tried to read the new book he'd borrowed from the library, but there was a paragraph about talking mice, so he tossed that aside. He doodled on a piece of paper, but soon his circles and zigzags connected into a head, and then into the body of a cartoon mouse, as if his hand had a mind of its own. In frustration, he crumpled up the paper.

Adam didn't like to admit it, but in particularly lonely moments like this, he wished he had at least one friend. A friend who was a real person, just like him— someone to swap stories and joke with, the way other sixth-graders did.

He sat in his room until the empty silence, without the usual scratching noises Speedy made, became unbearable. He shuffled back downstairs, looking for something to distract himself.

Outside, the early afternoon sun hung lazily behind puffy autumn clouds. The first brittle leaves had begun to litter the sidewalk. Adam decided to sweep the leaves from the front of the store—a boring task, but his uncle would appreciate it.

First, though, a quick snack.

The croissants behind the counter still looked fresh enough. Adam started to reach for one with raspberry jelly. He halted.

On the counter, the snow globe had changed. The glass dome was no longer empty, but contained a tiny, snow-covered city.

Adam examined the snow globe. The cityscape within looked just like New York. He thought of J.C. Walsh's snow globe again.

Great things await you. Fantastic things.

Adam batted away the voice. He carefully inspected the snow globe again. It still looked like an ordinary snow globe, the kind sold in toy stores or tourist shops. Adam shrugged and gave it a shake. Sparkling snow confetti swirled inside the glass.

Then a single, real snowflake landed on the back of Adam's hand.

CHAPTER FOUR

AN UNEXPECTED HOLIDAY

Adam now stood in the middle of a busy, snow-covered sidewalk. Around him, snowflakes fell steadily between enormous flashing neon signs and glittering buildings that towered over both sides of the packed street.

He recognized this place. It was Times Square, the center of New York City. Somewhere beyond the crowds of people bundled in winter jackets and scarves, bells jingled in the freezing night air. The gigantic billboards above featured red-white-and-green advertisements.

Adam clutched the snow globe in his hands, wondering how he'd managed to get himself here, in the middle of December. He was still only wearing his long-sleeved T-shirt and jeans, an impractical combination for the new weather situation. The icy wind bit into his exposed skin like a set of sharp teeth. He stumbled backward and accidentally jostled several people carrying shopping bags. One of them dropped a candy cane in the shuffle.

"Watch it!" another person snapped.

Adam stammered an apology. He turned in all directions, unsure what to do next. The snow and crowds, not to mention the sudden shock, were disorienting.

"Hey kid!" shouted a voice behind him.

He spun to face a dark-skinned girl in a gray cloak. She was a head taller than Adam but looked no older than nine or ten, and she carried an armful of long, white-and-green-striped candles. With her free hand, she pushed back her thick curly hair and spoke again.

"Are you nuts?" she asked. "Where's your jacket?"

"Don't h-have one." Adam's teeth chattered, and his mouth hurt to move.

"Where's your ma and pa?"

Adam shook his head. "Gone," he said shortly.

The girl's eyes softened. "Come with me."

Adam hesitated. Although he normally wouldn't follow a stranger, he was in no position to refuse right now. He could barely feel his fingers, and it wouldn't be long before he became like one of the immobile paper snowmen plastered on the store windows nearby. The girl seemed confident enough, so he trailed after her.

She led him down the snowy streets, weaving expertly left and right through the crowds. After they'd gone a couple of blocks, Adam realized they were heading east. His senses returning, he began to take in more details of his surroundings.

That was when Adam noticed there was something not quite right about the city.

The street signs were humped and shaped like little blue bowler hats instead of normal green rectangles. The cars that passed were nothing like the sort he was used to; they looked more like boxy wagon carts, reminiscent of those seen in black-and-white movies. As a clanging streetcar made its way uneasily among them, he realized the advertisements on the billboards and windows seemed off, too, their art style reminding him of cartoons he saw once from Uncle Henry's collection of vintage newspapers.

But everything else seemed normal enough. They passed large shop windows lit with colorful, flickering lights, and tall office buildings more than twenty floors high. Laughing families bustled out of stores with armfuls of glossy, gift-wrapped boxes.

The two passed the giant Christmas tree at Rockefeller Center. Adam and his uncle had visited the tree in previous winters. Every December, the city lit up the enormous evergreen for the holiday season, and it attracted millions of visitors. The tree stood tall and wide, about ten stories high, and it glowed with enough shimmering lights to brighten a dozen ballrooms.

The girl in the cloak kept going. The quick pace warmed Adam up somewhat, though his shoes were wet and squishy from the slush, and his arms had goose bumps that felt as large as pumpkin seeds. His hair was also damp from the snow. To forget how cold he was, he concentrated on the puffs of fog his breath made in the air.

The girl walked briskly along until they arrived at a quiet alleyway away from the main streets. The narrow space was shielded from most of the snow. A worn canvas bag lay on the ground next to a makeshift shelter that contained a bed of thick blankets and pillows. Behind the bed was a mountain of candles.

The girl stooped down and rummaged through the bag. She pulled out a wooly brown blanket and tossed it to Adam.

The blanket was scratchy, but it instantly protected Adam from the cold. His lips were numb, but he managed a shaky "Th-thanks."

"Don't mention it," said the girl. "My name's Francine. What's yours?"

"I'm Adam."

"Say that again?"

"Adam," he mumbled louder.

"Okay, Adam. You're lost, aren't you? I can take you to the cops, but I can't go inside the station with you."

"No, I know where my home is . . ." The last thing Adam wanted was to explain to the police how he'd magically transported across the city—and apparently across an entire season.

"Are you from the orphanage?" asked Francine.

"No, I live with my uncle."

"Where?"

"The Lower East Side," Adam answered. Then, because he was curious, "Do you—do you *live* here?"

"Don't be silly. This is just a temporary spot to store my inventory, before the snow gets bad. Times Square is full of customers around the holidays, see?"

Francine turned to the pile of candles and began to brush away the snow at the edge of the heap. The care with which she did it reminded Adam of how he handled Speedy.

Adam's curiosity must have been apparent, because Francine explained, "They're from a factory in a nearby town. My friend got them for me. They make a good buck in the winter." Francine held a candle out for Adam to see.

The candle was half the size of Adam's arm, and the color of vanilla with green stripes. He carefully touched the smooth, waxy surface of the candle, and could tell the quality was superb. It smelled like flowers.

"Want one?" asked Francine. "Only costs ten cents each."

Adam shook his head. "I don't have any money with me."

"Your loss, then." Francine snatched the candle back.

"So . . ." Adam looked at the girl. "You don't have any family?"

Francine's eyes narrowed. "You're not going to report me, are you?"

Adam didn't know what to say. He thought of

inviting Francine to stop by his place. The bakery had plenty of leftover bread and pastries, and the place was always warm.

As he was thinking of the best way to bring this up, Francine challenged, "What's *your* story?"

"Me?"

"Wandering around New York in the middle of winter without a coat?" Francine crossed her arms. "Let's hear the story behind that."

Of course, Adam didn't know any more than Francine did.

"I'm not sure," he said. "But I have to get home."

"You're lying," Francine said flatly. She studied him closer. "Although, you're not a bad actor. A little more practice and you could be like Shirley Temple." She straightened. "Well, I've got sights to see and candles to sell. You know how to get back from here, kid?"

Adam was about to say yes when he noticed a crumpled newspaper on the ground in the alley. For a moment, he stared at the front page of the damp paper in stunned silence. The print date read:

DECEMBER 10, 1935

When he looked up again, Francine was giving him directions on the quickest way to get to the Lower East Side by drawing a map in the snow.

"Just keep heading east till you hit Second Avenue. Avoid this area here—crowded because of all the Christmas shows going on—"

"That newspaper," interrupted Adam. "Is that newspaper real?"

"What?"

Adam couldn't speak. His mind raced. He thought of the street signs, the clanging streetcars.

Francine looked at him. "You okay, kid?"

Adam had almost forgotten about the snow globe, which he carried absentmindedly. It suddenly became heavy in his hands, the glass as cold as an ice cube. He peered under the blanket. To his surprise, the snow globe's cityscape had disappeared. All that was left inside was the snow confetti. The snow globe looked exactly the same as when Adam had first found it in the attic earlier that day.

He held up the snow globe to his face. The snow confetti swirled inside the empty glass. All of a sudden, he was no longer standing in the snowy street but was back in the warm, dry interior of the Biscuit Basket.

Nobody else was there. Outside, crispy autumn leaves rolled across the sun-dappled sidewalks. Adam's sneakers, however, were dripping with snowy slush. The wooly blanket was still draped around his shoulders.

If you've ever shocked yourself with electricity, you'll agree it's a very painful experience. That is why people are discouraged from standing outside during thunderstorms, for if lightning does strike you, you'll be frizzled like a human pancake. The surprise that Adam felt after his sudden trip was comparable to an electric shock, only instead of leaving behind a scorched burn, the experience left him standing motionless in great confusion.

Adam didn't know how long he stood there afterward. He hardly noticed when Uncle Henry came home; he merely shook his head when his uncle asked if he was feeling ill. Convinced that Adam was worried about the money problems, Uncle Henry made them a pot of his famous rice pudding and told Adam not to fret.

"I got a good deal on the candelabra," the baker reassured Adam. "If business picks up a little, we shouldn't have to worry about rent for several months."

The twelve-year-old still looked troubled, so Uncle Henry sent him to bed early.

That night, Adam couldn't sleep. He tossed and turned, and his mind raced endlessly. The mysterious events, the wintery city, and the words of the man in the raincoat played on repeat in his head.

He didn't know it, but across the city, another person was wide awake at the same time. Like Adam, this individual tossed and turned. Unlike Adam, he kept muttering under his breath in a most ominous fashion, *"The snow globe . . ."* But we'll get back to him a little later.

CHAPTER FIVE

PAST, PRESENT, AND FUTURE

Some people don't believe in magic. Others find magic in the most ordinary things.

Baking, for example, is a bit like magic. You take several different ingredients: flour, salt, and baking soda, all of which by themselves taste nasty. Not even a hungry dog likes to lick raw flour or baking soda off the floor.

But after mixing these simple ingredients together, adding a pinch of water, and heating the mixture in the oven, you'll find these ingredients come together to form something greater than the sum of its parts. You now have warm, delicious bread that not a single person or animal in the world would turn up their noses at— especially not a hungry dog.

After his strange experience with the snow globe, Adam wasn't sure what he believed. The whole scene in Times Square lingered in his mind, too vivid to be a dream. Francine's wooly blanket was neatly folded and tucked under his bed. Yet the globe remained blank for the rest of the week—long enough for him to start questioning whether any of it had been real. The first thing Adam did each day was to look at the snow globe, which he kept close on his nightstand. He sped home after school each afternoon to see if the snow globe's contents changed, and popped in every hour on the dot before bedtime. The last thing Adam did each night before he went to sleep was to check the glass ball again.

It remained empty.

All he knew was that the clue to solving the snow globe's mysteries lay with the man in the raincoat. He searched the phonebook for J.C. Walsh. There were at least fifty people with the name J. Walsh listed in New York City. The closest he could find to a J.C. Walsh was a "Josefina Charlotte Walsh," a person who, when he called, sounded to be a woman in her eighties.

No progress there.

He also tried to keep an eye out for Francine on his way to and from school, but in a city as big as New York, it was akin to trying to find a single salt grain in a sugar jar. He even stopped by the Hole to ask Victor if he or any of the other residents ever knew any orphans by the name of Francine. No luck.

He knew it was no use. Francine had apparently lived over sixty years ago, after all, so how would he possibly recognize a seventy-year-old version of her? Even as he wondered that, part of him refused to believe he'd actually traveled back in time. Because time traveling was impossible. Not only that, but everything he'd seen with Francine had been as colorful and as lively as New York City today, and everyone knew the past was supposed to be like the black-and-white photos in history textbooks or lifeless exhibits at museums—something distant and not easily relatable.

Adam tried his best to recall whether his parents had ever mentioned the magical snow globe. The only memory that came to mind was a fuzzy incident from when he was four, one year before the big accident. He had been sitting in the living room next to his mother, and had been watching his father argue with several other adults in the room. It had been a lively argument—heads shook, voices were raised, fingers stabbed the air to make a point. A man with a bushy beard kept waving his hands, while an elderly woman and Adam's parents tried to calm him. Adam didn't remember what the argument was about, but he did recall his father pointing to the snow globe on the bookcase.

At bedtime, his father used to tell Adam stories about faraway places, of tradesmen in Asia, wizards in Europe, and hidden treasure caves in Africa. His father had vowed on his name that the tales had been firsthand experiences from his and Adam's mother's travels. Magic stories.

As soon as Adam remembered this, he got an idea. He ventured upstairs to the attic again and rummaged in his parents' box. He opened up the topmost atlas in the pile. The edges were worn, and the pages had pencil markings—notes his parents had taken. Dates of visits were scribbled above destinations. Four more atlases lay piled underneath the first.

Adam read every note throughout every atlas in the box until his eyes nearly crossed from fatigue. His parents had traveled to every single continent, across more than eighty countries. Yet there wasn't any mention of a snow globe anywhere.

Magic stories. He went back downstairs, shaking the cobwebs and dust from his hair, feeling defeated.

CHAPTER SIX

ACT I, SCENE I

Unbeknownst to Adam, approximately one hundred years ago in New York City, there lived a bright magician who had no doubts whatsoever about magic. He lived and breathed magic. His name was Elbert.

Elbert Walsh.

Elbert was seventeen. From a young age, he dreamed of becoming a stage magician. He longed to join the ranks of Houdini and Thurston—men who had astounded half the world with their illusions.

Elbert's parents, a pair of hardworking immigrants from Ireland, wished their son would pursue a more "practical" career instead. Elbert's mother mended clothes and sold used tea leaves in the streets. His father worked the docks at the shipyard, and often came home with sunburns and bruises. Elbert and his parents lived in a crowded apartment shared with two other families, with only one bathtub and a tiny crackling stove that didn't always work.

But Elbert refused to give up his dreams of stardom, despite his parents' protests. Over the years, he slowly saved up pocket change for magic supplies by doing odd jobs. But most of his earnings came from street performances. For privacy, he would practice his act in the narrow alleyway behind his apartment. Then, hour after hour, he roamed the neighborhood, producing roses out of hats and making bottle caps disappear. He pushed his fluttering pet dove from his sleeves. He transformed green handkerchiefs into red ones and back again.

And he kept his eye on the Silk Hatters.

The Silk Hatters were an outstanding local group of five magicians, each with a unique ability: the Escape Artist; the Levitator; the Hypnotist; the Mind Reader; and the Vanisher. During their performances, the members each wore a signature black silk hat.

One day, word spread that the Hypnotist had fallen ill with smallpox, and the troupe was searching for a replacement. The first chance he had, Elbert signed up for an audition on the piece of parchment posted outside the theater.

On the day of his audition, he used his savings to rent a suit. He bathed, combed his hair, and, slightly nervous, entered the empty theater where the rest of the Silk Hatters were judging applicants.

The enormous theater swallowed Elbert up. He stood motionless, soaking in the scene. After his eyes adjusted to the blinding stage lights, he looked out into the vacant seats and imagined himself performing a real show in front of a full audience. Thunderous applause echoed in his mind, along with crowds chanting his name. *Here he is, folks, the Magnificent Elbert!*

Someone in fact was shouting from the front row.

"Hurry up and start already!" yelled one of the Silk Hatters, jolting Elbert back to reality.

He was barely two minutes into his first act before the Silk Hatters began to scoff at his performance.

"What good is a color-changing handkerchief?" clucked the Levitator, a particularly pompous middle-aged man with a cherry-red nose. "We're looking for *real* talent here."

Elbert's magic dove act was also met with scornful laughter.

"This bores me," shouted the Escape Artist, a round-faced man with bulging muscles. "I have seen enough doves that appear out of nowhere to last me a lifetime! Let's cast the votes already. Gentlemen—"

"Don't forget *woman*," piped up the Mind Reader, a petite lady whose silk hat covered nearly half her face.

"—all in favor of accepting this young man into our troupe, say aye. Otherwise, say nay."

Nays were echoed by all four troupe members.

Elbert grasped for one last chance. "I have a good act," he promised. He started re-creating the rose-from-the-hat trick. The Silk Hatters booed. Flustered, Elbert accidentally dropped the rose. His pet dove escaped from his sleeve to pick it up.

"Still boring," fake-snored the Levitator.

To top it all off, the Vanisher, a shrewd, tiny man who highly resembled a rat—he even had whiskers on his face—produced a ripe tomato from his pocket and chucked it at the stage. The tomato splattered against Elbert's head.

Poor Elbert, he could only stand in stunned silence, tomato dribbling down his golden hair, as the troupe members howled with laughter. The Levitator wiped away tears.

"You'll never be worth anything, boy," he said, his shoulders shaking from laughing so hard. "Not to worry. Most men aren't destined for fame."

"Or women," added the Mind Reader.

Heartbroken, Elbert left the theater with a pit in his stomach. He sat on the curb the rest of the afternoon, too embarrassed to go home and admit his failure to his parents. His pet dove gently pecked at his hand to cheer him up.

The pit in Elbert's stomach eventually burned with anger. He kicked his scruffy shoes against the uneven pavement. Who did the Silk Hatters think they were? He would show them.

That evening, with stale tomato bits in his hair, he roamed aimlessly down the streets until he noticed a clockmaker's shop not far from the busy marketplace. As he stared through its windows at the steadily rotating hands of the pocket watches and the rhythmic, back-and-forth pendulum of a grandfather clock, an idea popped in his head.

He ventured into the shop. He was greeted by the soft tick-tocking of the numerous timepieces that lined the dimly lit shelves, as well as the gentle aroma of lavender. Clocks of all shapes and sizes surrounded him— long clocks in handsome dark wood, mantel clocks with enamel faces, brass and silver pocket watches, wristwatches. It was clear the clockmaker took great care in his handiwork. Each wooden item was delicately carved and free from even a speck of dust. Their fine details shone in the soft glow of dozens of green-and-white-striped candles that sat in sconces mounted along the walls. Elbert realized these candles were responsible for the lavender smell.

The clockmaker sat behind the desk in the corner, examining a wristwatch through a magnifying lens. He was an ancient man, with tufts of feathery white hair and a weathered face. The clockmaker peered up at Elbert and asked in a soft voice, "May I help you?"

Elbert replied he was looking for the best pendulum money could buy, though he kept his lips sealed about the pitiful amount of money he actually had in his pockets. He told the clockmaker he wanted something that could "hypnotize and wow an audience."

The clockmaker seemed to ponder Elbert's request,

his eyes slowly sweeping over the magician as if reading him. At long last, he nodded, dusted off his hands on his sweater vest, and introduced himself as Santiago. If the old man noticed the tomato drippings in Elbert's hair, he made no mention of it. Santiago moved slowly and talked slowly, but Elbert could tell each step and every word was carried out with a sense of purpose.

Santiago led Elbert to his collection of clock parts. There were silver chains, tiny bells, dials, windup keys, and pendulums.

"I believe this will suit your needs," the clockmaker said, showing Elbert a sleek black case.

Inside the case lay a fat, golden pendulum, its thin chain nested snugly in the velvet cushion. Elbert immediately felt himself drawn to the pendulum, as if it were a magnet. He touched the gold. It was solid, but not flashy. It had an irresistible appeal.

"I obtained this long ago from a fellow clockmaker," said Santiago with a smile. "I daresay he did not know its true value, though that's not necessarily a great loss. I don't have much use for it, myself."

"How do you know for sure it can hypnotize people?" asked Elbert.

"Look at yourself. You're entranced by the gold, yes?"

True. Elbert asked for the price. It was far beyond what he could afford.

"Come now, cheer up," Santiago said gently, upon seeing Elbert's dejected look. "Tell you what, I'll lend you the pendulum. All I ask in return is that you help out in my shop every evening until your debt is paid, and it will be yours to keep."

"Truly, sir?" whispered Elbert.

The clockmaker placed the pendulum around Elbert's neck and gave him a steady smile. "Life goes round and round like a clock, my friend, but our individual roles in the cycle are brief. What good is our precious time if we don't use it to help each other out?"

Thanks to the clockmaker's golden pendulum, Elbert's magic acts improved tenfold. Within three months, he had risen among the ranks of the magician world as a promising hypnotist. He went from performing in the streets to performing in taverns and shops, until finally he was performing on stages in crowded theaters.

Word quickly spread about "Elbert the Excellent" across the city. Journalists and crowds swarmed around the magician after each show with questions. Soon, people all up and down the East Coast had learned of Elbert and his magnificent ability to make a person do anything on command.

Skeptics also speculated about the logic behind the magic act.

"Humans are simply attracted to the pendulum's gold finish," explained a stodgy professor in a lecture to his students. "The magic itself is not real. They just see the gold and become mesmerized like fools."

Real magic or not, Elbert became wildly successful. So successful, in fact, that the Silk Hatters approached him a few months later. They again had another open spot in their troupe, because the Levitator had accidentally fallen thirty feet during a performance and broken his leg in two places. The remaining members of the Silk Hatters told Elbert they'd be happy to welcome him to the group.

To which Elbert laughed out loud for a solid ten seconds, responded, "Abracadabra," and left them in the dust.

Elbert never forgot his deal with the clockmaker. Each night after his evening performance, he graciously made his way through the usual crowd of devoted fans and dutifully went to Santiago's shop to help out. Over the months, he'd learned quite a bit about clock making and the mechanics behind it—how to clean a clock, how to fix a broken pocket watch, how to replace the gears.

He had also picked up a few other tricks from Santiago, like how to use lavender oil as a healing scent, and how to make long-lasting candle clocks that told the time with each melting stripe. "Candles are no ordinary things," the clockmaker liked to say with a wink. "You can light many more candles with just one, and the original flame never weakens." On Elbert's eighteenth birthday, before lighting the candles on Elbert's cake in that very fashion, Santiago also taught him how to create perfect buttercream frosting.

The shop itself often hinted at something unusual beyond everyday clock making. Elbert could've sworn, on several occasions, all the clocks stopped ticking at exactly the same time, only to start again when the old clockmaker appeared at the doorway. There were also instances when the hands on the grandfather clock moved not forward, but *backward*, until it struck six o'clock when in fact it was near ten in the evening. When Elbert pointed this out once, the clock hands jumped and promptly reset themselves to show the correct time. Santiago simply gave Elbert a mysterious smile afterward and went back to polishing a pocket watch.

The old clockmaker also had a few unusual ideas about time itself. One wintery evening, as they watched the beginnings of a snowstorm through the shop window, Santiago told Elbert about the time touch.

"Legend says three pieces of time fell from the sky ages ago," said the clockmaker. "A piece of the past, a piece of the present, and a piece of the future. They floated across the land, drifting like clouds. Everything they touched experienced time differently from how we normally do."

"How so, sir?" asked Elbert.

Santiago held up a mantel clock. "You and I experience

time as a line, from one minute to the next." He then adjusted the knob so that the minute hand rotated backward. "But with a piece of the time touch, we would experience time not as a line, but as an entangled web. Cause and effect would not be as clear."

Elbert didn't follow, but decided not to interrupt.

"Very few people have stumbled upon pieces of the time touch, and even fewer have been able to recount its magic," Santiago said cryptically. "Those that have say the three pieces of time scattered across the world. When they finally settled, each became locked inside a unique object that maximizes the piece's power. People have searched centuries for these objects. The power contained in these fragments of time is not to be underestimated. It is said that with a piece in hand, one can *control time*."

"What kind of objects are we talking about?"

"Allegedly all sorts of things—lockets, flasks, jewelry cases. Even clocks. Imagine that. Of course, only a slim handful know what—and where—the true objects are: the few who've stumbled upon the real thing."

"Do *you* know what the real objects are?" whispered Elbert.

"I have some guesses," the clockmaker replied with a twinkle in his eye.

"What do you mean by 'control time'?"

"If the stories are true, each piece supposedly allows you to control a part of time: the past, the present, or the future. But what the time touch can do to a person is incredibly dangerous. There are rumors of people losing their minds after coming into contact with one of the pieces. People competing for ownership. Even killing one another. Yes, you may be able to control time . . . but it might ultimately be that time controls you."

A gust of wind rattled the window. Elbert waited for the clockmaker to continue, but the old man went back to fixing a broken pocket watch and refused to speak about the time touch any further for the rest of the night.

The next evening, Elbert brought up their conversation from the day before. He wanted to know more about the time touch.

"How is it dangerous, you ask?" replied Santiago. "Anything that has the power to reshape how we think is dangerous, Elbert. It can stretch us to our limits and send us down a slippery path. Ultimately, the time touch changes our very character—either for the better or for the worse. That is why whoever stumbles upon a piece of the time touch must not share it widely, lest the rest of the world fall under its influence or try to compete for it."

The answer didn't satisfy Elbert. "And how would one even know if they stumble upon a piece of the time touch?" he questioned. "Does it rattle or glow?"

"It's an ancient magic, invisible like the wind." Santiago picked up a rag and started polishing the clocks on the shelves. "But it's unmistakable. It draws you in, becomes part of you. Someone who does magic for a living like yourself would sense it right away, even if you couldn't identify it. Moreover, with the time touch, time itself would begin acting strange in your presence."

Elbert felt almost foolish asking, but he blurted, "You've seen it, haven't you, sir? The time touch?"

Santiago smiled. "An answer for another time, perhaps. For now, let me ask you this. Which would you rather? To be able to know the future or to travel to the past?"

"Being able to know the future," Elbert answered promptly. "Then I can see if I'll ever be famous enough to perform alongside the Great Houdini and all the best magicians."

"Mm, is that so?" The clockmaker carefully wiped the face of a cuckoo clock until it gleamed in the surrounding candlelight. "The time touch would take it one step further, I'm afraid."

At the time, Elbert simply wrote off Santiago's words as cryptic nonsense. It wasn't until much later that Elbert would understand what the clockmaker meant.

CHAPTER SEVEN

BUTCHERS AND BITTERSWEET BONBONS

Nine days had passed since Adam went on his trip and met Francine.

It was after midnight. He could hear his uncle snoring in the living room. But Adam couldn't fall asleep—he was especially jittery that night, his mind a frenzy of thoughts bouncing off one another like rubber balls. After another hour of insomnia, he quietly shut his bedroom door and turned on the lights.

The snow globe sat on his dresser. The inside of the ball remained empty, just as it had been for the past week. He tapped on the glass. Nothing.

Francine's wooly blanket still lay under Adam's bed. The blanket served as a token of Adam's sanity. As long as it was there, it meant he hadn't been dreaming.

Maybe if he wished hard enough, the scene in the glass would change again. He closed his eyes, then opened them.

Suddenly, he sat upright.

The same snowy cityscape from before had appeared inside the snow globe, the layer of snow confetti lying on the bottom of the glass. It was as if the snow globe was just yearning for a shake so that the confetti could dance and cascade like a real snowfall.

After thinking for several moments, Adam made his decision. He quietly rummaged in his closet and put on his fraying winter jacket and scarf. He also wrapped the wooly blanket around his shoulders for good measure.

Then he shook the snow globe.

This time, Adam ended up on a quiet street corner in daytime. There was snow on the ground, but it wasn't the same soft, fluffy sort that comes from a new snowfall. Instead, the snow was icy and hard, the kind that comes after being trampled a few days. It crunched under his shoes like frosted sugar.

A street sign pinpointed Adam in the Upper West Side. It was the kind of neighborhood he had only seen in passing, one with carefully trimmed hedges, shoveled sidewalks, and magnificent townhouses. Uniformed doormen stood at the polished gates that lined the tidy blocks. The glitzy, wagon-like cars parked outside and the unusual number of people wearing top hats indicated that he was no longer in 1999.

A yell from an alleyway across the street caught

Adam's attention. Next to the alley was a store with a fancy green awning above that read in fine cursive letters, BRICK'S BUTCHER HOUSE. Hanging in the store window was an array of plump sausages, Italian-style deli meats, and enormous roast chickens big enough to feed a family of two for a whole week.

A small girl sped out from the alley. With a jolt, Adam recognized her as Francine. Two seconds later, a large man in a bloodstained apron who Adam guessed was the butcher ran out after Francine, yelling at the top of his lungs.

"Come back or I'll have you dead, you dirty child!"

Several passersby in fur coats stopped to stare. Francine kept running, her gray cloak billowing behind her, but the butcher gained on her with lightning speed. He caught up to her and yanked on her hair, pulling her to a stop.

"Hey!" shouted Adam, running over. "Let her go!"

Francine was wincing in pain as the butcher held her in a headlock, but she managed to glance at the boy who had joined them.

"Adam?" she gasped.

The butcher's teeth were stained yellow, and his breath smelled of spoiled meat. He threw an angry scowl at Adam and snarled, "Of course. I remember you worked in pairs."

With one of his meaty hands, the butcher clamped

Adam's arm. Adam dropped his snow globe on the side-walk. Thankfully, the thick glass survived the fall.

Adam struggled to break free, but the butcher's grip was like steel.

"Let him go!" snapped Francine. "He has nothing to do with this."

"I've had enough of you thieving kids stealing from my shop. Rotten orphans—I know that's what you both are." Here the butcher leaned in and gave them a smirk. "That means nobody'll miss you."

He forced them back down the street. Francine shouted at the butcher, "You idiot, he's not the boy you're thinking of! Tito's sick with polio!"

But the butcher didn't seem to hear. He was laughing maniacally to himself, between muttered phrases of "Boil 'em brats in hot water" and "Hang 'em out to dry like salami."

Although Adam was small for his age, he knew how to use his size to his advantage. At school he often slipped away from bullies' grasps like a block of butter. Here, he took a deep breath, then threw himself flat on the sidewalk. The sudden force of his weight yanked the butcher to a stop. Adam seized the opportunity and gave a mighty kick to the butcher's shin.

The butcher howled in pain and released both kids.

"Run!" shouted Francine.

The butcher swiped at them. Adam rolled out of the

way just in time. That was one good thing about being small: you could swerve and dodge your opponents easily. He hastily picked up the snow globe. The tiny cityscape was still inside. He tucked it under his arm.

Francine also aimed a kick at the butcher, releasing another howl from the large man, before she and Adam hurried down the street. They bolted around the corner and didn't stop running until they were several blocks away. Francine found a shortcut, and they streaked through the narrow alleyway. They finally stopped next to a crowded playground, thinking the butcher likely wouldn't go after them in front of all the watchful parents. There the two caught their breath.

The first thing Francine panted was, "Where'd you even *come* from?"

"No idea," Adam said truthfully. He rubbed his arm, where the butcher's grip had left a painful mark. He realized he had left the wooly blanket back at the scene. At least his snow globe was safe. "Why'd you steal from him?"

"I didn't *steal*. I was looking through his trash for scraps." Francine revealed three links of red sausage she had hidden in her canvas bag. They smelled spicy and still looked fresh. "I *should've* stolen from him," she spat. "He overcharges for his meats anyway. Not that he'd ever sell anything to me."

Adam didn't say anything. He and Uncle Henry had seen their small share of thieves in the bakery—a muffin here, a doughnut there. But Uncle Henry always let them go. He had once told Adam, "If they're desperate enough to steal food, you leave them alone. No one ought to go hungry."

"I'm sorry about your friend Tito," Adam said.

Francine stiffened. She pretended to be busy adjusting her cloak.

"Tito and I are more than friends," said Francine after a long silence. "He's like family. He's an orphan like me. Same age, too." She kicked at the snow. "I always said ten was a lucky number, but guess not."

Part of Adam couldn't believe Francine was only two years younger than he was. The girl acted so much older.

He had learned in history class about polio, the crippling disease that had left numerous children paralyzed and bedridden. It had been eradicated in the United States in 1979. There was no doubt about the snow globe's time traveling properties now.

"Who are you *really*?" Francine blurted, changing the subject. "How do you pop up out of nowhere? Are you a magician?"

Adam didn't know how to respond.

"That snow globe has something to do with it, doesn't it?" Francine said knowingly as she stared at the glass orb in Adam's hands.

Surprised, Adam nodded. He hesitated, then said, "It kind of transported me here. It did the same thing on that day we first met, the day you lent me your blanket, however long ago that was."

"You mean two days ago?"

Adam blinked. "Um, I guess so," he replied.

He expected Francine to give him a weird look or to call him crazy, but instead he saw her eyeing the bright neon on his sneakers. "So what," she said flatly, "you're from the future?"

"Yes."

Francine shook her head and said, "I knew it," before hoisting her canvas bag on her shoulder. Adam was surprised by her nonchalance, as if time traveling was as ordinary as rainy days. "Well, thanks, kid."

"For what?"

"For saving my hide back at the butcher's."

She turned and started to leave.

"Where are you going?" asked Adam, startled.

"Home," Francine answered without looking back. "Tito and everyone's waiting. You wanna come?"

What choice did Adam have? There must have been a reason the snow globe brought him right to Francine both times. So he followed her up the street.

They walked briskly in silence. After a while, Francine spoke about Tito some more.

"Before he got sick, he'd find all sorts of stuff in the streets—rings, unused movie tickets, boxes of half-eaten chocolates. We'd sell them with the candles. That butcher's place was our favorite spot for special days. Birthdays, Hanukkah, Christmas, Easter . . . We wouldn't take much, just unsold leftovers that he'd tossed in the bin in the alley. And when we *did* swipe the occasional hunk of meat from the window display, we'd take just enough to get by."

"You said Tito got you those candles from a factory, right?" said Adam.

"No, that's my other friend Daisy. And yes. The factory is in Daisy's hometown. It makes tons of candles, and throws away the rejects. Daisy brings bundles of them to orphans like me so we can resell them and make some extra money. She says the factory owner gets mad at her, but seems like a shame to have the candles waste away, y'know, all because of a missing stripe or what have you."

"Where is this factory, exactly?"

"Not far, in a small town just north of the city."

They walked several more blocks until they reached a noticeably less wealthy part of town. Here the brick buildings were fenced with rusty chain wire. Several windows were boarded up.

Francine led the way to what looked like an abandoned warehouse. She crouched and pushed open a small, ground-level windowpane in the side of the building. It was wide enough for them to slip through.

"I don't know about this," Adam said. He knew what Uncle Henry would say if Adam had willingly entered an abandoned warehouse.

Francine rolled her eyes. "It's just me and the other kids here. We don't bite."

Adam heard distant laughter from somewhere inside. He also thought he heard a radio playing.

Reluctantly, he slid through the open window. The floors and walls were dusty and bare, but there was plenty of sunlight, and the room looked like someone had attempted to make it more welcoming. A row of chipped flowerpots sat next to the wall, along with shiny pebbles, stacks of colorful dinner plates, and piles of random items, including several worn picture books, paper dolls, and a small silver cassette player. Five cardboard boxes had been pushed together to form a makeshift table, complete with a thin sheet that served as a tablecloth. On the opposite side of the warehouse, rows of sleeping bags and blankets were set up. A group of children were giggling across the large space, absorbed in a game of marbles, while a dusty-looking gramophone played nearby.

"We fend for ourselves here," Francine said. "Some of us sell newspapers. A few shine shoes—those businessmen types downtown love them shiny. Although lately, times have been tough for them, so we haven't had as many customers," she added.

"But what do you eat?" Adam couldn't help asking.

"Like I said, unwanted leftovers," Francine answered easily, as if they were talking about the weather. "We know where to find the best leftovers in New York City.

French fries, steaks, you name it. You won't believe how many people throw away entire plates of food. We pool our money together, and sometimes we save up enough to buy hot pretzels with mustard to share on birthdays."

Once again, Adam wanted to tell her about his uncle's bakery. Maybe he could bring a cake back next time.

He followed Francine to the far corner of the warehouse, where someone had stacked a wall of crates. She motioned for him to stand back, then took out the sausage links and disappeared behind the crates. She came back a moment later, her hands empty.

"We made a place for him over there," she explained, "so the rest of us don't get sick too."

Adam realized she was talking about Tito. "He should see a doctor," Adam said.

Francine shook her head. "The hospitals are full of polio patients these days. Ones who can pay. Orphans like us rarely get seen."

Francine walked over to a pile of items, rummaged through it, and produced a thin, red, rectangular box. She lifted the lid and held the box up to Adam.

"Special treat?" she asked. It was clear she wanted to change the subject.

Adam peered inside. The candies in the box were round and patterned like peppermints, except they were transparent like glass and had scarlet and black spirals. Francine wasted no time. She eagerly took two pieces and popped them in her mouth. She winced, then grinned.

"Try it," she urged Adam. "Daisy makes the best sweets in the city."

Somehow Adam doubted that. He had been taught as a young kid not to take sweets from strangers. But Francine had trusted him enough to invite him to her secret home, and she looked at Adam expectantly. So, against his better judgment, he tried a piece.

The candy tasted terrible. It was bitter and salty. Adam almost spit it out, but Francine said, "Give it a few more seconds."

The flavors made Adam think of thunderclouds and broken floorboards—and black crows, which had gathered in a cluster at his parents' funeral. His second-grade teacher had taught the class that a group of crows was called a murder of crows. Murder. Death. The thought dampened his mood considerably, and he wondered what he'd gotten himself into, following a strange girl to a warehouse in a completely different era.

Then, with a twang, the flavor changed. All at once the candy tasted wonderful, like vanilla, strawberry, honey, and something fizzy melted together. Adam bit into it. The pieces crunched between his teeth. He found himself grinning from ear to ear, just like Francine.

"Told you," Francine said with a nod. "Bittersweet Bonbons, Daisy calls them. Made with her special formula. Once you get past the bitter part, you taste heaven."

"Who is Daisy, exactly?"

"I told you, she's a friend. We met downtown a while back. She works as an apprentice for one of the city's most famous candy shops, and she's moving up the ranks." Francine sounded proud. "Did you know, she doesn't have a family either? Her family disowned her for some reason or another. She left home to become a candy maker."

"That's sad . . . but also neat." *Bittersweet* was the right term for it.

Francine looked at her hands. "I wasn't always an orphan, you know. I had a family too, until I was seven."

"Oh." Adam didn't know what to say. "What happened?"

"We were at the carnival," Francine answered shortly. "There was an accident. Here, have more."

Adam and Francine each enjoyed two more Bittersweet Bonbons. Adam found it akin to taking fever medicine whenever he got sick—one quick gulp, with a pinch of the nose, and then shortly after, you feel much better than before.

"How old are you?" Francine asked, swallowing the last of her candy.

"I'm twelve," said Adam.

Francine reached into her canvas bag and counted out twelve white-and-green candles. She handed the bundle to Adam.

"A thank-you present," she explained. "For helping me escape that butcher."

Adam hesitated.

"Plenty more where those came from. Take them."

Adam thanked her. "I'll try to help Tito," he murmured. "In the future, they have a vaccine for polio. Not a cure, exactly, but almost."

Francine suddenly sounded weary. "Don't," she said simply.

"What do you mean?"

But Francine clamped her mouth shut and refused to answer. She avoided Adam's eyes. Instead, her gaze fell on the snow globe.

"Your snow globe city just disappeared," she pointed out.

Adam glanced at the tilted snow globe in his hand. He noticed too late the confetti sliding behind the glass—and the missing cityscape inside.

When he looked up again, Francine was gone. In fact, the whole warehouse had disappeared. Adam was back in his bedroom, standing next to his dresser, his hands clutching the candles and the snow globe. He could hear Uncle Henry still snoring in the living room.

Afterward, Adam lay wide awake in bed for a long time. Then, in the quiet stillness, he suddenly realized something.

In the piles of random items along the wall at Francine's, there had been a silver cassette player.

A cassette player. Adam no longer listened to cassette tapes—hardly anyone did in 1999, thanks to CDs—but even he knew that such an invention was *completely* out of place in Francine's time.

Its presence meant one of two things:

Either Francine was a time traveler too, or Adam was not the first person to have traveled through time to visit her.

CHAPTER EIGHT

THE CLOCKMAKER'S SECRET

One month after Elbert Walsh turned eighteen, he discovered something truly remarkable.

He had just emerged from the stage with his trusty golden pendulum. It had been a particularly noteworthy performance. He'd hypnotized the mayor into a deep trance, and the audience had watched in awe as the mayor began doing whatever Elbert instructed him to do. The mayor did three cartwheels and yodeled for the audience for two minutes before falling out of the trance, with no recollection of what had happened.

As usual, the cheering crowds gathered around him in the lobby. Journalists jotted down notes about the spectacular performance for the next day's press and pelted the magician with questions.

"Elbert the Excellent," cried a reporter with slick black hair. "Is it true your pendulum is pure magic?"

Elbert had heard this question numerous times. He merely winked in reply.

"Elbert the Excellent, are you going to duel the Great Houdini?" someone else shouted.

"Elbert, Elbert! What's your favorite color?"

"Elbert the Excellent—what's your secret?"

"Sorry," answered Elbert. "A good magician never reveals his secrets."

He managed to escape the crowd. Outside, Elbert put on his spring cloak and headed for Santiago's shop. It had been almost a year since he'd purchased the golden pendulum. The old clockmaker had told him his debt was more than repaid, but Elbert enjoyed working alongside Santiago, so he kept going back.

That evening, Elbert noticed the outside of the shop was looking worn. But the inside was as well kept as ever. He walked through the door and breathed in the familiar smell of polished wood, metal clock gears, and lavender-scented candles.

"In here," came Santiago's hoarse call.

Elbert met him in the back of the shop, where the clockmaker kept customers' timepieces in need of repairs. The old man was in the middle of inspecting a broken wristwatch.

"How was the show?" asked Santiago.

"Very good, sir," answered Elbert, dangling the glistening pendulum around his thumb with a wink, then slipping it back into his pocket. "I've been asked to perform in Philadelphia next month."

"That is marvelous. I always saw great potential in you." Santiago let out a long cough.

"Are you all right, sir?"

"Yes. Dreadful allergies." The clockmaker sniffed. "Try not to catch hay fever like me."

In the last few months, Elbert had grown increasingly worried about Santiago's health. The old man's back made him stoop so low, he was half the height of the grandfather clocks.

That night, Santiago had not one, but five more coughing spells. Each time, Elbert watched helplessly. He offered to get a glass of water, to get medicine from the drugstore. The old man refused again and again.

The two were storing away the pocket watches for the night when Elbert raised the question that tumbled uneasily in his head.

"Santiago," he said. "What's going to happen to the shop once you . . . retire?"

"My clocks are my life. I will not retire."

"No, sir, I meant what'll happen should you become ill and . . ." Elbert trailed off uncomfortably.

There was a long silence. "Why do you ask?"

"Who's going to run the shop? Take on repairs for your customers? What will happen to all these wonderful clocks you've made? There are lots of valuables here, sir. You can't let them go to just any random person. It'll be a waste if they're not appreciated."

"Ah." Santiago smiled. "I am fond of all my works, Elbert, but there are really only two valuables in this entire shop. Three, if you count the pendulum in your hand, but that belongs to you."

The old man slowly moved across the room to the metal safe snuggled inside the back wall. Elbert had never seen what was inside the safe before. He watched with curiosity as Santiago rotated the combination lock, then reached inside and retrieved a small item draped in velvet cloth.

"I have not shown this to another living soul," the clockmaker said in a hushed voice.

He removed the cloth to reveal a delicately carved box. It was the color of chestnut, with a golden crest in the front and four short legs at the base. Shiny gold bands embossed the edges.

"Is it a music box?" asked Elbert.

"It's more than just a music box," Santiago said with a knowing smile. He paused, and Elbert knew he was choosing his words carefully. "This special device is bewitched."

"Bewitched?"

"See how it has no windup key? That's because the music doesn't play on command. It plays only on . . . certain occasions."

"What occasions?" asked Elbert, intrigued.

But Santiago refused to answer. "Ownership of this

music box is not for the fainthearted, for its music will bring them trouble and grief. It is not for those who seek *reasons* behind why things happen."

Elbert touched the music box. A tingle shot up his fingertips, all the way to his shoulders.

"Careful," murmured Santiago.

"Where'd you get it?"

"That's a story of its own. The short version is I obtained it after long years of searching, and after gaining the trust of its previous owner. It has only played twice for me. Twice is enough."

The clockmaker's riddling way of speaking started to irritate Elbert, but his annoyance was quickly replaced by worry when Santiago let out another long cough.

"What's the other valuable item?" asked Elbert.

Santiago slowly retrieved a battered journal from the safe. The soft blue cover had hundreds of wrinkles and creases. "My research," Santiago said simply.

He put away the music box and the journal, and locked the safe door behind them.

"To your original question about me and my shop—do not worry about the future, my friend," said the clockmaker. "Focus on the present first, and the rest will fall into place."

Before Elbert left that night, however, Santiago added, "But if I do die tomorrow, please make sure my two valuables stay protected."

"I will," promised Elbert.

CHAPTER NINE

CANDLEWICK

By now, of course, Adam was fully aware the snow globe had some kind of special property. Twice, with the snow globe in hand, he had inexplicably traveled to a different location in New York City, and a different date altogether.

Even so, he hadn't told his uncle about the snow globe or any of his adventures. For one thing, Uncle Henry had a no-nonsense approach when it came to magic. When Adam was younger and they read fairy tales together at bedtime, Uncle Henry would add his own commentary to the storylines.

For example, "'The Three Little Pigs said—' Hm, *said* must be a metaphor, since pigs don't speak English . . ."

Or, "'Rapunzel let down her long hair, and the prince used it to climb up the tower—' which can never happen, by all means. Why, poor Rapunzel's neck would snap in her effort to support the prince's weight!"

Or, " 'Hansel and Gretel found a house made of cake and candy—' although a house like that in real life would attract enough ants and animals to eat the whole thing in a day. Besides, it would be impossible to walk inside. Have these writers seen how easily cake crumbles?"

What would Uncle Henry say about time traveling, aside from sending Adam to the psychiatrist?

Besides, Adam was protective of the snow globe. It might have been the simple fact that it belonged to his late parents. He didn't have many items—much less valuables—that belonged to them. After they died, adults in crisp suits and briefcases had mentioned most of his parents' items would be taken away, and used legal words like "repossession of property" and "unfulfilled expenses" that Adam didn't fully understand.

It might also have been the unspoken feeling that a magic powerful enough to break the strings of time was best kept secret. Time traveling was no ordinary thing. Adam was smart enough to know that if too many people found out about the snow globe, total chaos would ensue.

Then there was a third, deeper reason, which he didn't want to admit to himself. It was the idea that if the snow globe could really get him to travel back in time regularly, maybe he could somehow travel back to before his parents died and warn them not to get on the plane that fateful day. He didn't dare to bring his hopes up. But hope is a funny thing, springing forth despite our best efforts to squelch it, like a bag of popcorn kernels bursting in the microwave.

Meanwhile, Halloween was fast approaching. This year, the ingenious holiday where kids dress up as monsters and ghosts in exchange for free candy fell on a weekend, which meant extra time for everyone to ramp up the festivities. Haunted house tours, discounted costumes, and candy sales exploded up and down the streets. The Biscuit Basket also prepared for the event by advertising special jack-o'-lantern cakes and bat-shaped chocolate cookies.

The bakery attracted more customers than usual, due to the bright array of candles displayed there each night. Adam's uncle had helped him set up the candles from Francine, which Adam simply said he'd found in the attic. Every evening, the bakery was aglow with a dozen flickering orange lights and the soothing scent of flowers—"like lavender and something tangy," Uncle Henry had said after sniffing with his powerful baker's nose. Multiple people stopped by to gawk at the display.

"These candles were a brilliant idea, just brilliant," Uncle Henry told Adam after they sold another box of bat-shaped cookies. "Candlelight really gives the place a special feeling, doesn't it?"

Adam agreed. How strange it was that candles were one of the only things appropriate for display at both happy events and sad events—ideal whether it was a birthday, a holiday, or a funeral.

As he helped serve the stream of new customers over

the next few days, he began to notice a repeated face in the crowd. There was a tall, thin man in a black suit situated outside the bakery each day. The man had dark hair that matched his suit, and a distinct, pointy chin, above which sat a permanent scowl. He stood just outside the window, peering inside, always in the same spot, and was gone after a few moments.

On one of the evenings, after Adam delivered leftovers to the Hole, he glimpsed the same man skulking in the shadows of the alley, watching him. When the man saw Adam staring back, he vanished into the alley.

On Friday, Adam told his uncle about his suspicions.

"A stranger who follows you?" repeated Uncle Henry.

Adam nodded. "He hangs outside the bakery. Mostly in the evenings." He thought he might've seen the stranger once before heading to school in the morning, too, but he couldn't be sure.

His uncle stopped mixing a bowl of cream to give him a look of concern. "Has this man ever spoken to you?"

"No."

"Hm, I'll keep an eye out. Meanwhile, be sure to stay in plain sight of other people." Uncle Henry went back to mixing the cream and said, mostly to himself, "Probably just a competitor trying to case out the place, now that we're doing well. We'll show them!"

On Saturday evening, the day before Halloween, something strange happened. It didn't have to do with the stranger in the black suit, nor did it have to do with the teenagers dressed up as mummies who littered the sidewalks with toilet paper, infuriating every neighbor on the block.

But it did have to do with—yes, you guessed it—the snow globe.

When Adam went to bed, his eyes widened. His heart nearly jumped out of his chest.

The snow globe on the dresser had changed. Inside the glass was a miniature town on a hilly, grassy countryside.

Adam examined the tiny piece of scenery for several long moments. Then he went downstairs—"I forgot something," he responded to Uncle Henry's questioning gaze in the living room. Downstairs in the bakery, Adam snatched four leftover pastries (he had a feeling Francine might like the ones filled with cheese) and hurried back upstairs. In his room, he threw on his winter jacket and scarf just in case. Then he put the pastries in a paper bag and picked up the snow globe with his free hand.

He gave it a shake.

As expected, he found himself on a grassy hill, the same hill that was inside the snow globe. The sky was a deep lavender, and the air felt like late summer. It was much too warm for winter clothing. Adam unzipped his jacket and folded his scarf under his arm.

The hill overlooked several more hilltops. A small town was sprawled across the last of them, its houses like miniature red-and-white toy blocks glued together. Behind them loomed an ominous gray building, its smokestacks spewing matching gray clouds into the sky.

The only logical thing to do was to walk toward the town, and that's what Adam did.

As the sky darkened, the streetlights in town flickered on one by one. When Adam reached the outskirts, he realized these were no ordinary streetlights. They were shaped in the style of old-fashioned lanterns. A wrought-iron lamp dangled from a spiraling pole at the top of each post, and they used candles instead of lightbulbs. He inspected the closest streetlamp, where yellow flames flickered above a chunky candle sitting within the glass cage.

For a moment, Adam wondered if he had traveled way back in time, to an era without electricity. But as he made his way farther into town, he saw the homes were the usual type of suburban houses found in many parts of the country: redbrick, two stories, medium garage, white picket fence. The front yards were trimmed; some had pockets of flowers. The place reminded him of his own early childhood, back before he moved to the city with Uncle Henry. He remembered the wide-open spaces, the fresh smells of mowed grass and the neighbor's sunflowers in the summertime.

By now, many of the houses had turned on their lights,

and Adam could see the activities going on behind the windows. In one house, a woman spoke on the telephone while a teenage boy and toddler sat in front of a thick TV, their eyes glued to a black-and-white cartoon show. In the adjacent house, an elderly woman chopped vegetables in the kitchen. One street over, two boys were playing basketball in their driveway. Somewhere, a dog barked.

None of these houses attracted Adam. No, what specifically caught his attention was the fifth house on Oak Street. Soft, eerie music floated through an open window on the first floor of the square, redbrick house. It was the kind of melody that made Adam think of graveyards and starless nights.

The music drew Adam closer to the window. Inside, he saw a boy in an aviator helmet fiddling with a wooden music box on his bed, looking frustrated. When the last note faded, the boy in the room looked up. Straight at Adam.

"Who are you?"

Adam stumbled backward.

The boy came to the window. He looked to be about Adam's age, athletic with skeptical blue eyes. "Who are you?" the boy repeated. "Why are you spying on me?"

"I-I wasn't," Adam stammered. But he was caught red-handed. He confessed, "I was just listening to your music box."

He quickly turned to leave, but the boy in the aviator helmet shouted, "Wait!"

The boy opened the window wider and motioned for Adam to return. "Don't go yet," he said with a glance down the street. "Stay for a while, I won't bite. Are you new in town? My name's Jack, by the way." The boy offered a smile.

Adam could tell Jack was one of those popular boys in school, the kind who had no trouble making friends.

"I'm Adam," he said hesitantly. "I'm from New York City."

"Really? My dad and I go there sometimes on the train, so we can see movies. The theaters there are fantastic. Did your family just move out here?"

"No. I'm only visiting."

"Who are you visiting? I know pretty much everyone in town."

Adam hid the snow globe behind his back, along with the bag of pastries. Francine had to be around somewhere. "Just—a friend. I should go."

"Come on, what are you in a hurry for?" said Jack. "You were practically spying on me a minute ago. It's not my aviator helmet that's scaring you, is it?"

Nobody had ever warmed up to Adam so quickly, much less joked with him. He flushed and didn't know how to respond. He changed the subject. "Can I see your music box?"

Jack pressed his lips into a tight line. "I don't know. . . ."

But the boy must've thought Adam would leave

otherwise, because he went to retrieve it. He returned, holding the music box stiffly, with his arms outstretched, like the box was a bomb that might go off any second. "There, see it?"

It was a nice music box—handsome chestnut wood with a golden crest. Strangely, it didn't seem to have a windup key anywhere. Adam reached across the windowsill for the device to take a closer look, but Jack jerked it away.

"Where'd you get it?" asked Adam, thinking again of the haunting music it made.

"My dad gave it to me a few months ago for my eleventh birthday. It used to belong to his dad. My grandpa."

"Oh," said Adam. That must be why Jack was being so careful with it. "Its music is . . . interesting."

"Yeah," Jack said shortly. He carefully placed the music box on his desk. Next to the box lay a half-finished model airplane and an empty pewter candlestick.

The rest of Jack's room was simple but neat. Along the wall near the window stood a bookshelf filled with rows of aviation magazines and completed model airplanes. The same magazines were piled on the dresser and on the nightstand in the corner. Above the nightstand was a calendar, open to August 1967.

Adam had traveled thirty-two years into the past.

Jack saw Adam eyeing the airplanes. "My dad got those for me," Jack said. "The Boeing 707 is my favorite. Only took us two hours to put together." He let slip a proud smile. "I want to be a pilot one day. What about you? Do you like airplanes?"

"No," Adam answered immediately, a bit too loudly.

Jack's smile flickered. "Not everyone has to like the same things," he said, sounding slightly hurt.

"I know, I . . ." Embarrassed, Adam's voice trailed off. There was a moment of silence, before it was broken by Jack again.

"I have a question," Jack said, studying Adam for a moment. "Are you from Asia?"

Adam was used to questions about his appearance. "I was born here," he answered. "My mom was originally from China and my dad was American, though his ancestors came from Germany. My parents met doing charity work in Europe. Opposite sides of the world—I contain half the world in me," he added jokingly, hoping to impress Jack.

Jack gawked at Adam. "That's neat. You know the Supreme Court's only just overturned that marriage law, don't you?"

"What marriage law?"

"The law that bans people with different skin colors from marrying each other."

Adam bit his lip. It was definitely a weird thought that if his parents had lived thirty years earlier, they might not have been allowed to marry.

"I think the rule was silly," Jack went on. "It's like

saying people with yellow hair can only marry other blonds. Or people with freckles can only marry other freckled folks. That's what it boils down to, really."

"Yes," Adam agreed. "So . . . where are your parents?"

"I live with my dad. He's at work." Jack nodded down the street.

Adam glanced in the direction Jack was looking. He saw the gray building again, much closer now, with its large smokestacks still blowing out great clouds of smoke.

"What is that place?"

Jack snorted, though not unkindly. "You don't know what *that* is? You really aren't from around here, are you? That's the candle factory—the so-called jewel of Candlewick. Candlewick's Candles Corporation."

So Candlewick was the name of the town. Adam cracked a smile at the unusual name. He made a mental note to look up the town once he got home. He had no idea where he was on a map, but he couldn't risk giving himself away by asking Jack for specifics.

Instead, he asked, "Why is it the jewel of Candlewick?"

"Well, the whole town is crazy about candles," Jack said. "That's how we make our living. My dad even named me after that nursery rhyme about candles. The one that goes,

"Jack be nimble, Jack be quick,
Jack jump over the candlestick."

77

"Is that why you have a candlestick on your desk?" Adam asked.

Jack laughed and said, "Good one," even though Adam hadn't been joking.

"You can't find candles like the ones made here anywhere else in the world," continued Jack. "Everyone in town works there. It makes a ton of money, so people think the factory's the jewel of Candlewick. But it's not, not really, since most of that money ends up going to the Gold Mold."

"What's the Gold Mold?"

"Not what—*who*," corrected Jack. "The Gold Mold is the owner of Candlewick's Candles. Richest and nastiest guy in town. He overworks everyone and yells at them all the time. He even keeps part of the money he's supposed to pay them."

"That sounds awful."

Jack nodded. "He wears this stupid gold pendulum around his neck wherever he goes, like he needs to flaunt how much money he has with dumb jewelry. That's why I call him the Gold Mold. Shiny on the outside, full of mold and ugly stuff on the inside. Well, maybe some actual gold on the inside. Did you know he eats gold flakes with his dinner?"

Adam grimaced. He knew lots of bakeries in New York that used gold to give their pastries extra sparkle, but to him, eating gold seemed about as appealing as eating paint or toilet paper, not to mention an extravagant waste.

"He's the meanest, greediest man there ever was." Jack frowned. "This was before I was born, but when he first took over the factory, he found out his little sister had been giving away candles to poor kids to sell. They had a big fight about it. People say he was always jealous of his sister—she aimed to be successful without relying on the family business, and that made them rivals, I guess."

Something about this story sounded awfully familiar to Adam. "What happened next?"

"His sister made desserts—sweets and chocolates and stuff. A few years later, he bought up all the sweet shops in town, to prove he was good at things other than candles. But he wasn't. Once he became the shops' new owner, he sold the candy at five hundred times their original price. Now no one can afford it. I only get candy when I go to New York City with my dad."

"What does the Gold Mold do with all the unsold candy?"

"He eats it all! His own son doesn't even get any. Although," Jack said with a shrug, "I've never met the Gold Mold's son in person. People say he's sort of a recluse." He clasped his hands and glanced down the street again.

Even though Adam knew it was none of his business, he asked timidly, "Why doesn't your dad and everyone else find another job if the Gold Mold is so awful?"

Jack scrunched his eyebrows under his aviator

helmet. "I don't know. My dad says he wants to leave Candlewick, but he never does. It's like he suddenly forgets about the things the Gold Mold does. Like one day, he accidentally did an order wrong and got smacked by the Gold Mold's cane. My dad had a huge bruise on his arm. He swore he was quitting that night. But when the next day came, he couldn't even remember how he got the bruise. He didn't believe me when I told him."

Adam suggested quietly that a bad memory was likely at play there. But Jack shook his head.

"My dad's as sharp as they come," he argued. "He's brilliant—look at all the model planes we've built. Anyway, this is one of the only jobs around, and there aren't many options for veterans like him. My grandpa wasn't happy when he found out my dad was working at Candlewick's Candles. Said he could forgive but never forget what the owners did. Grandpa was a bit of an odd duck, but he told me the best stories. He never approved of the factory—"

A loud whistle pierced the air. Jack bolted upright and craned his neck to look out the window.

"Shift's over," he said nervously. "My dad'll be home soon. Do you think . . ." He glanced at Adam. "Could you stay with me just a bit longer? Just until my dad comes back for sure?"

"Sure, okay."

Adam understood. He used to wait for his parents to come home too when he was little. He'd count down the days on the calendar. Five more days until they finished delivering medical supplies here; four more days until they returned from building houses there; three more days, two until they were done exploring the mountains of Switzerland.

The last countdown had been two hours, forty-three minutes. Then had come the untimely accident.

Adam waited silently alongside Jack, who watched the street with the intensity of a hawk. After a while, figures slowly appeared at the slope of the hill. Adults in crinkled shirts and grubby khakis shuffled up the street, their faces vacant and drained. Each adult continued walking past and paid no attention to the two boys. A few cars drove past, old-style vehicles that Uncle Henry would've called *vintage*.

With each passing person, Jack craned his neck farther. His knuckles grew white as he pressed them into the windowsill.

"No sign of him yet?" Adam asked after the eleventh worker had passed.

Jack shook his head without speaking.

Adam felt bad for Jack. If his own father had ever worked for someone like the Gold Mold, or had come home with bruises from work, he'd be worried, too. He also noticed that Jack's eyes kept darting surreptitiously to the music box.

Suddenly, Jack's face lit up, and his shoulders collapsed in relief. "Dad!" he called.

Down the street, a middle-aged man was trudging up the slope. He had gray hair and smile lines underneath his tired eyes. When he heard Jack call, he waved.

Jack disappeared from the window and emerged from the front door of the house. He ran down to greet his father. As he did, he called over his shoulder to Adam, "Thanks for waiting with me!"

Adam raised his hand. "You're welcome," he faltered, but Jack had already sprinted down the street out of earshot. Adam stood still and watched as father and son embraced on the sidewalk. The father swung Jack onto his shoulders. Jack spread out his arms as if he were a bird or, more likely, an airplane. Something tugged inside Adam's chest.

He stepped back to look at the front door: 18 Oak Street. Adam memorized the address.

It was perhaps good he did, because when he turned to look at Jack and his father again, they were gone. The town was gone. He was back in his own room. The snow globe sat lopsided in his hand, the swirling snowflake confetti just beginning to settle inside the empty glass.

On Monday morning, Adam woke up extra early. He trekked to the local library before school to research the town of Candlewick. He'd wanted to go sooner— the minute the snow globe brought him back home, in fact—but it had been late on Saturday when he returned, and then on Sunday the library had been closed. More-over, it was Halloween. Business at the Biscuit Basket was booming, and Adam was kept busy helping Uncle Henry. As he'd handed out free candy corn to each customer, he thought back to the Gold Mold buying out every candy shop in Jack's town. One thing was certain—his own uncle would never sell out to the Gold Mold, no matter how much he was offered.

At the library, Adam breathlessly looked up the town of Candlewick. It was indeed a real place, located several dozen miles north of New York City near the Hudson Valley. According to the last U.S. census, the town had around three hundred people.

Then Adam paused in the middle of his research. He did a double take.

"No way," he whispered, rereading the passage that had caught his attention. Shivers crawled up his spine.

The town's namesake candle factory had burned down in 1967, killing most of its workers.

CHAPTER TEN

IN WHICH BAD LUCK PREVAILS

Not long after New Year's Day in 1909, Santiago fell deathly ill. Shortly after, he passed away.

It was a curious incident, though nobody was there to witness it. The clocks in the shop all stopped ticking at the time of the clockmaker's death. Only when someone found him the next morning did the clocks start working again.

The funeral that followed was small. Several neighbors and some of Santiago's loyal customers were in attendance. Elbert delivered a heartfelt eulogy he had written in memory of the clockmaker.

At the end of the funeral, Elbert lit two of Santiago's homemade candles, one on each side of the clockmaker's casket. The sweet scent of lavender filled the small room.

That was the last time anyone would see Elbert for a while.

His performances stopped for several months. The

streets whispered and speculated about the magician's sudden disappearance. Nobody knew where he had gone.

Several months later, Elbert made a brief reappearance one spring evening when he at last felt ready to stop by the clockmaker's familiar shop again. When he entered, he was aghast to find city officials clearing out Santiago's possessions. Clocks, pocket watches, springs, tools, and various gears were piled inside crates.

"Stop!" shouted Elbert. "What are you doing?"

The city officials said they were reclaiming the shop. "Santiago didn't leave an heir in his will," one of them explained. "All his items belong to the city now."

With some light pleading—and a little hypnotic help from his golden pendulum—Elbert managed to secure the two valuables he'd promised Santiago he'd take care of. Then he disappeared once more, the music box and notebook under his arm.

While the rest of the world puzzled over Elbert the Excellent's retreat from the stage, the young magician was undergoing a change. After Santiago's death, he no longer found enjoyment in magic tricks and hypnotism. Instead, he became fixated on the mysteries of the time touch, just like his mentor.

In his new studio apartment at the edge of the city, he immersed himself in Santiago's scrawling notes. The pages were filled with scientific diagrams and personal anecdotes, theoretical ideas and half-finished sentences. Each night, with his pet dove perched on his shoulder, Elbert slowly and painstakingly rewrote the notes into a notebook of his own, filling in the blanks with his best guesses, until finally, weeks later, he had pieced together the nearly illegible diary.

From this exercise, he gleaned some insight into Santiago's past. The clockmaker had apparently had a rough childhood. There were bits and bobs about stowing away on a ship from Argentina with his sister as children, about life on the streets in London, about his emergence as a renowned clockmaker in the United States. There were recurring notes about a motherly figure he simply called "the Governess." From what Elbert could tell, the Governess had adopted Santiago and his sister back in London, and for a few golden years, they'd all been happy. But then the Governess's sudden death had led the clockmaker to an obsession with time and the story of the time touch—and ultimately, to his quest to track down its legendary pieces.

Elbert also confirmed an amazing but not-so-startling fact in Santiago's notes: the clockmaker had indeed been partially successful in his efforts.

London—December 8, 1845
I visited the hermit in the clock tower one last time. He agreed to hand over the enchanted music

box, as he finally deemed me worthy of being
its new owner. I believe he felt a bit sorry for me.
That, or he was showing signs of having finally
been driven mad by its magic, same as its previous
owners were rumored to be.

All the years I've spent listening for stories
and all the miles I've traveled were worth it. I now
have one of the most valuable items in existence.
No words can describe the piece. It is like the
most wonderful thing in the world spun with every
terrible nightmare that exists.

I am still trying to determine whether it can
be controlled in some way, or whether it simply
operates of its own accord. One thing is certain:
ownership of this item will be a burden. It's far
better suited for one who lives a dark and lonely
life, who has no light left to share in the world.
Such an existence would lift the burden, to be sure,
but it's not a life I desire. I must be careful not to
fall down that path.

Someday, my turn will come to pass along this
valuable piece to another trustworthy soul. Until
then, I hope to complete what I've set out to do.

Although Elbert was unsurprised to learn Santiago owned a piece of the time touch, he found it rather curious that the piece was inside, of all places, the music box. He had yet to see evidence of the box's magic. Aside from the tingling sensation he had when he'd first touched it, the music box seemed like an ordinary thing. No matter how he tinkered, toyed, and fiddled with the box, he couldn't get it to open. It remained tightly shut, day after day, month after month. Santiago had told him it only played on certain occasions, but he never said what those occasions were.

So Elbert went back through Santiago's transcribed notes seeking clues. He spent several weeks ruminating on a particularly enigmatic verse the clockmaker had written:

There are three parts to the time touch, locked in
three separate objects:
One in which all is foretold,
One in which lie gifts of gold,
One in which past days unfold.

One piece of the time touch lay, of course, in the music box. Which piece it was, Elbert couldn't say. He deduced it was not the third, since a diary entry late in Santiago's life specifically mentioned it as something that eluded him.

New York—July 10, 1904
   The one in which past days unfold—the most
important piece of all. My guess has always been
that the object is a clock of some sort. The hands

*would go backward and allow the user to go
back through time. For fifty years and counting,
whenever a customer brings in a watch or timepiece
that needs fixing, I've kept a keen eye out for such
an item. I've written to my colleagues in other
cities, I've watched the international papers for
news of strange timepieces. But to no avail. I worry
I've been mistaken.*

Elbert also suspected, though Santiago never wrote or spoke of it explicitly, that the clockmaker had a second piece of the time touch in his possession: the one in which lie gifts of gold. He thought back to his days performing onstage. The golden pendulum Santiago had sold him had always been extraordinary—perhaps a tad too extraordinary. Elbert recalled how whenever he'd used it, time seemed to stand still briefly, not just for the person he was hypnotizing, but also for himself. But that was where the magic seemed to end. If the pendulum did contain a piece of the time touch, Elbert had yet to see its true powers (much like the music box). Nonetheless, he made sure he kept the pendulum close to his heart as he continued his research.

Perhaps what haunted him most was the last and final page in Santiago's diary, written in a shaky hand:

*It is my own folly that I expected to have time
and energy to continue my search at this stage.*

Despite my best efforts, I failed to locate that most important piece—the one that I am certain would have allowed me to save the Governess. Even so, my work has resulted in a good and interesting life, and I think of what is to come when I am gone.

I met a bright young magician the other day. Full of potential, with a good heart. Worthy of the responsibility.

Like the hermit in the tower, it is time for me to pass on the legacy.

I believe in you, Elbert. Keep safe what you've been given, and I wish you luck in finding what eluded me.

The research kept Elbert busy. At first, he saw no one, talked to no one, and barely went outside, unless it was for a quick run to the market for some bread and fruit.

But bread and fruit cost money, and it soon became clear to Elbert that he would have to engage with the world if he wanted to eat and continue his quest. To pay the bills, he sold homemade lavender candle clocks, exactly as Santiago had taught him. Day and night, the studio apartment was crowded with pots of wax, lavender, and batches of long, white-and-green-striped candles that burned precisely one stripe every hour. They lasted twice as long as the other candles on the market, and were touted to have healing powers thanks to their gentle lavender scent. The candles became immensely popular. (It helped, too, that a small group of Elbert's most ardent fans from his magician days promoted the candles wherever they could.) Soon, Elbert had loyal customers returning to his apartment each week, from fishmongers to teachers to wealthy doctors in three-piece suits.

"Several of my patients said these cured their headaches," a doctor told him after buying five dozen. "I give them to everyone who comes to see me now."

A banker told him the candles kept time better than his own pocket watch.

Another buyer asked, impressed, "Where'd you learn how to make these extraordinary candles?"

"A wise clockmaker taught me," was Elbert's simple answer.

Each week, after paying his expenses, he sent half his remaining earnings to his parents, who did not know much about their son's research but were nonetheless thrilled he had left the fickle show business for a more stable career.

Then one evening, a little after midnight, the music box opened for the first time. Elbert woke to a strange, eerie tune. The music was short yet long, simple yet complicated. When the melody ended, the music box closed by itself, and remained shut.

The very next morning, Elbert's pet dove flew headfirst into the window. The poor bird died instantly.

A year after that incident, the music box opened and played for the second time. Elbert had just returned from visiting his mother in the hospital, where she was staying due to fevers and weight loss. That very afternoon, his mother passed.

When the music box played again, several weeks later, Elbert immediately tried to close the lid. But while the music box wouldn't open before, now it wouldn't shut no matter how hard he pushed, not until the entire melody had finished.

Three days after, a letter arrived stating his father had been crushed to death by an anchor at the docks.

Now, Elbert was not a superstitious person. You'd think a magician might be especially susceptible to the blurred line between reality and the mysterious, but Elbert was not. He had never dreaded Friday the thirteenth. He didn't blink twice when he'd accidentally broken a mirror in his youth, nor did he trouble himself with the many black cats that had crossed his path over the years. But now, the meaning of the music box loomed over him like a shadow, and warnings from Santiago echoed in his head. He began to have doubts.

"Must not let anyone else have this bewitched object," he vowed. Such an object could drive people insane with its premonitions—starting with himself. He thought of chucking it to the bottom of the ocean, or burning it altogether in his fireplace, but Santiago's many years of chasing the object guilted Elbert.

So he kept the music box buried inside the wall in the back of his closet. That's where he hoped it would quietly lie, until his own death.

Then had come the candle theft.

Over the years, the popularity of Elbert's candles had caught the attention of a wealthy businessman. He appeared at Elbert's doorstep on an autumn evening, wearing a decorative three-piece suit and clutching an elegant walking stick.

"Elbert Walsh, I presume?"

"That's me."

"Pleased." The businessman had hair the color of salt and pepper, and two long, heavy eyebrows, which rose in a scornful sneer as he glanced inside the small apartment. In a self-important tone, he said, "My name is Robert Baron. Word on the street is that your candle clocks are more precise and last longer than any other on the market, and that they apparently possess healing powers."

"Er, yes—" began Elbert.

"I'll get to the point," the businessman interrupted. "I wish to buy your candles."

"Certainly, sir. How many would you like?"

"No, no, you misunderstand me," huffed the businessman. He gave an impatient sigh. "I want to buy the rights to your candles—goods, formulas, and all. I'll brand them and make an empire out of them."

"I'm sorry, sir. The formula is not for sale."

Although Elbert didn't know it at the time, this businessman was a particularly greedy fellow. So greedy, in fact, that he had five companies to his name, all of which had been acquired by a mix of bribery, theft, and, failing those, any means necessary, no matter the cost.

In order to convince Elbert to give up his candles, Robert Baron tried the first tactic: bribery.

"I will pay you handsomely, of course," lied the businessman. "I will exchange most of my savings for the mere candle recipes. Four hundred dollars, not a penny less."

Although it was a lot of money (four hundred dollars back then was enough to pay Elbert's rent for a year), Elbert politely refused. His candles carried a lot of sentimental value for him. He had made an honest living with them, and the candles had allowed him to carry on Santiago's research and ruminations about the time touch.

A good businessperson isn't one who gives up easily. Robert Baron pressed on, "All right then, why don't I pay you *five* hundred dollars? Mm, no? How about six hundred?"

On and on this went, until the bid rose to fourteen hundred. It was more money than Elbert had made from a year's worth of stage performances, and infinitely more than what he made from selling bundles of candles.

"Well . . . all right," Elbert said after thinking it over. "On one condition. I want to be a full partner in the business. These candles mean a lot to me. I want to oversee the candle-making process, and make sure the candles meet the expectations of the man who originally inspired them."

"Yes, that can be arranged." The businessman gave a slick smile.

So Elbert signed the contract (which turned out to be fake). He handed the secret formula for the candles to Robert Baron (who turned out to be a snake). And it wasn't until the businessman left chuckling to himself that Elbert had an inkling something was wrong.

Half a week later, Elbert lost the rights to his candles. Stern-faced lawyers appeared at his door, warning him that if he sold one more candle, he would be arrested. Candles that Elbert *himself* had created.

Elbert angrily went to confront Robert Baron, but the man had many powerful connections from years of carrying out bribery and blackmail. Elbert was dragged away by the police in handcuffs before he could finish shouting at the crooked business tycoon, "You thief! What do you think you're playing at?"

"Sorry, boy," Robert Baron cackled. "It's only business."

Elbert spent three months in jail for disorderly conduct. When he returned to his apartment, he found everything covered with an inch of dust—and ransacked. Half his silverware was missing. His clothes littered the floor. His bookshelf had been overturned, and many of the books had been burned. To his dismay, this included his careful research on the time touch, along with Santiago's journal, the remains nothing more than blackened scraps of paper in the dusty fireplace.

Elbert dashed in a panic to his closet. He breathed a sigh of relief. The music box was still hidden safely inside the wall. Even after everything that had happened, breaking a promise to the clockmaker would have made Elbert feel guilty.

His brief moment of relief quickly evaporated.

One more item was missing from the mess: his prized golden pendulum.

CHAPTER ELEVEN

M IS FOR MENACING

Back at the bakery, Adam had limited free time. Word about the bakery had spread, thanks to the candles that had attracted many customers during Halloween, and, as the holidays approached, more and more people continued to stop by the Biscuit Basket. Some days, there was barely enough room to fit all the customers. Order after order of birthday cakes piled up in the kitchen. No breakfast pastries were left at the end of each day.

When Adam did find a few moments to himself, he slipped to the library in order to read more about the town of Candlewick.

It seemed the boy Jack had not been exaggerating about the candle factory's owner, who went down in history as a particularly notorious man. It was said none of the factory workers got time off, apart from one day at Christmastime each year. There had also been accidents at the factory, each one expertly swept under the rug.

In the few photos Adam could find, the Gold Mold faced the camera with a greedy smile on his chubby pink face, his enormous belly squeezed into an extravagant suit that was much too tight. In each photo, a golden disk hung from a chain around his neck.

One of those photos accompanied a newspaper article that went into great detail about the fire that had burned down the candle factory.

CANDLEWICK'S CANDLE FACTORY CATCHES FIRE
August 17, 1967

Factory headquarters of Candlewick's Candles Corporation, located in the town of Candlewick, New York, caught fire on the afternoon of August 15. Police reports indicate one hundred and ten people were caught in the flames and died, including the corporation's owner, Mr. Robert Tweed Baron III.

Candlewick's Candles was founded by Robert Baron III's grandfather, Robert Baron I, in 1913, and soon became known for its high-end, long-lasting scented candles that enjoyed an exclusive niche in the luxury home goods market. The factory was eventually due to pass to Baron III's heir, Robert Baron IV, who declined to comment for this article. Candlewick's Candles had been the town's largest employer, despite recent investigations into what some suspected were hostile working conditions at the factory.

No Candlewick employees or residents were available for comment at press time.

Although witnesses are currently scarce, the lead detective on the case is confident the blaze was caused by simple negligence. "The candles were carelessly stored, and they made a bad situation worse when the boiler blew," he said. "That thing should have been replaced years ago. There were also a lot of open flames from the candles, which we've learned has caused many smaller incidents in the past. You know, the only thing more dangerous than a candle factory is probably a needle factory."

The detective is also confident that were it not for an anonymous caller to the fire department, the number of casualties would have been far higher.

"More people would've died," agreed a volunteer firefighter. "We got a call about potential smoke just moments before the building went up in flames. We went over for a routine inspection and were able to get some of the workers out."

To date, there have been no charges filed against the Baron family.

From what Adam could piece together, the candle factory had been abandoned on the hill since the fire. Candlewick itself quickly became a ghost town.

Adam thought back to the candles Francine had. She'd mentioned they'd come from a small town just north of the city.

Adam tried to locate a list of the survivors' names, but couldn't find any. The curly-haired librarian gave him a puzzled look when he timidly asked if she knew where such records were kept, and soon began peppering him with curious questions, so he left in a hurry without the answers he needed.

On his way back home, an uneasy feeling lingered. He couldn't believe he'd met Jack the same month the candle factory burned down. Had they met mere days before the incident? What if it had been that same day?

If he could somehow go back in time again, he could warn Jack and the rest of the town.

But right now, there wasn't anything he could do. The snow globe stayed empty each night.

About two weeks after Adam's visit to Candlewick, a new visitor stopped by the Biscuit Basket.

It was almost closing time. Adam was wiping down the counter when the door opened.

"Hello, hello," greeted Uncle Henry in his usual cheerful manner. "What can I get for you, sir?"

"Something specific," a soft voice answered.

It was no normal voice, but one tingling with frost and danger—like a sharp icicle dangling from an awning and ready to break off any moment. It was this voice that made Adam turn. When he saw who stood in the bakery, he dropped his rag.

The tall stranger in the black suit stood before them. It was the same man who had stalked Adam in the streets, on the corners, and behind the windows of the bakery. Underneath his unkempt dark hair were a pair of long eyebrows that swooped down like two angry checkmarks. He had a thin, straight mustache above his pointy chin. His black eyes shifted to Adam.

Uncle Henry followed the man's piercing gaze. "Oh—yes, this is my nephew," he said with a friendly gesture. "Best helper ever. Can't run my bakery without him."

"I see . . ." the man said, his black eyes glinting.

Adam grabbed the nearest weapon—a wooden mixing spoon—and held his stance. But the stranger had already turned his attention back to Uncle Henry.

"I am looking for something specific," he said again in the same soft, dangerous voice. "Something that I've traced to this spot."

"You must mean my strawberry jam doughnuts," laughed Uncle Henry. "Here, try a sample. It will knock your socks right off."

"Um, Uncle Henry?" Adam spoke up quietly. "I don't think—"

The stranger in the black suit interrupted. "You misunderstand me. I do not want your silly sweets." His gaze fell on Adam again. "I am looking for a snow globe."

Uncle Henry finally began to sense something was odd. "All right, sir," he said. "I'd be happy to help you, but first, let's start with some introductions. What's your name?"

The stranger glared at the baker as if he were an irksome fly. "You may simply call me M."

"Nice to meet you, er, M. I'm Henry. You say you're looking for a snow globe?"

"Yes. Your nephew knows about it; ask the nice boy." M gave a fake smile that looked more like a sneer.

"Adam?" prompted Uncle Henry with a confused look.

Adam's hands grew clammy. "I don't know what he's talking about," he answered with a shrug. His instincts told him he must not let the stranger get the item.

"The snow globe." M's smirk wavered. "I believe you know *exactly* what I'm talking about."

"No, I don't."

"*Yes,* you do." M scowled and jabbed a long finger in Adam's direction. "Don't play games with me, you little worm. I've been researching this object for thirty-one years. You are the current owner of an extremely valuable item. Do you have any *idea* how many people have tried to get their hands on it?"

Uncle Henry stepped toward M and gave the stranger a warning look. Although Uncle Henry was shorter, he had a stockier build. M caught sight of Uncle Henry's strong baker muscles and backed away slightly.

"It seems we got off on the wrong foot," M said. "All I want is the snow globe. I am willing to pay handsomely for it. Name your price."

Uncle Henry faltered. He turned to Adam and murmured, "Do you think you could give the fellow whatever toy it is he wants, so he could leave us alone?"

Adam knew what his uncle was thinking: M had a few marbles missing, and the sooner they gave him the item he wanted, the better.

Except the snow globe was not just a harmless toy. Far from it. Furthermore, Adam did not trust M.

"Adam?" pressed Uncle Henry.

"Oh, you mean *that* snow globe," Adam said with a fake laugh. "Now I remember! Sorry, I broke that thing and threw it away a week ago."

"Listen to me, you imbecile!" spat M. "I'll skin you like a potato—"

Of course, making threats to a child right in front of his guardian is never a good idea. In an instant, Uncle Henry had grabbed the man's arm and was firmly guiding him out the door. M tried to resist, but he was no match for Uncle Henry's solid strength.

"You're making a terrible mistake," M hissed.

"Have a good day, sir. Please do not come back or I'll call the police." Uncle Henry slammed the door shut and twisted the lock.

M looked daggers at them through the glass. He pointed again at Adam and mouthed something before disappearing down the street.

"Are you all right, Adam?" Uncle Henry asked.

Adam found he was still rooted to the spot. He was also trembling. "I—I'm fine," he answered.

"Just another crazy guy, don't worry about him," Uncle Henry reassured Adam. "New York's full of bad seeds. They don't call it the Big Apple for nothing."

Adam didn't mention to his uncle that M was the stranger who had been stalking him. At least now he knew what the man was after.

And he had no doubt M would return.

CHAPTER TWELVE

THE GREAT BARON FAMILY

Adam remained watchful for the mysterious M. He made sure to keep the valuable snow globe hidden deep in his dresser. Even so, he checked on it every day to see if the landscape had changed. The glass globe remained empty.

He chewed on the facts. For one thing, he knew the candle factory had definitely closed down from a fire—a fire that had killed numerous people. It was his duty then, wasn't it, to warn Jack and the other residents of Candlewick? Perhaps that was why the mysterious stranger in the raincoat had shown him the way to the magic snow globe in the first place. Because what else could the snow globe be good for, if not to bring him back in time to help people?

Of course, what Adam wanted more than anything was to help his own parents. He wanted to warn them of their untimely deaths. But for anything to change, the snow globe had to change first. And that simply wasn't happening. Late in the evenings, he'd sit cross-legged on his bed with the snow globe in front of him, and he'd close his eyes and wish very hard that the inside of the snow globe would change to . . . he wasn't sure what, exactly. An airport? His parents' old townhouse in the suburbs?

He wasn't sure what he'd say if he *did* meet them again.

Then, four days after M paid Adam and his uncle a visit, Adam uncovered the snow globe to find it awaiting him with a new scene. This time, a tiny landscape of a cemetery stood inside the glass.

Adam's stomach churned. The sight of a graveyard was never a welcome sign. He thought of the burning candle factory and Jack. Something bad must have happened.

He did not pick up the snow globe.

It showed the cemetery all morning. Then, in the afternoon, the cemetery disappeared. Adam blinked at the empty glass, an unsteady feeling of regret in his stomach, the kind one might get after losing a twenty-dollar bill on the way to school, or after stepping in a pile of dog poop on the sidewalk.

Before dinner, the snow globe changed again. This time, a tiny hillside town stood inside the glass. Adam couldn't believe it. Candlewick.

For a moment, Adam stood still, paralyzed by

indecision. The doubts of continuing his adve[...] with the unpredictable snow globe washed over hin[...] was torn between staying in the safety of his invis[...] cocoon, and stepping out one more time in the name[...] curiosity.

His curiosity eventually won out. If he was seein[...] the town in the glass, it meant everyone there should be fine . . . right?

Adam took a deep breath, then gave the snow globe a gentle shake.

He felt a light breeze against his hand just before his room disappeared. In its place was a wide garden, bursting with bright flowers and neatly trimmed green hedges. The air burst with the feel of late spring and the sweet smell of early summer. Above him, wispy white clouds—the kind that looked like thin strips of cotton candy—drifted leisurely across the pale blue sky. The same warm breeze ruffled the patch of dandelions at Adam's feet, so that they brushed gently against his ankles.

At the edge of the garden stood a small girl examining a rosebush. The girl seemed no older than five or six, and wore a simple white dress. As if she could sense him, the girl looked up at Adam. She lifted a pale arm and waved. The girl was barefoot and held a golden pocket watch. A single daisy was pinned in her blond hair.

"Right on time," the girl said, smiling at him with round brown eyes. "Just like you said."

Adam didn't reply. He had no idea who the girl was or what she was talking about.

The girl motioned for him to follow as she brushed past him and led the way across the garden. That was when Adam realized the enormous house behind him. It looked more like a cathedral or a fancy hotel. Above the lofty windows and engraved walls, a weathervane in the shape of a candle perched on the slender roof. Adam had read in a book that the direction the weathervane points is where the wind comes from. Today, the wind blew from the southwest, behind the hills and the faint outline of the factory in the distance.

"Come with me," the girl called, before disappearing inside.

Adam hesitated, then followed her.

The inside of the mansion was even more impressive. The sleek, wood-paneled walls were decorated with framed paintings of picture-perfect landscapes, as well as portraits of the smiling little girl and presumably her brother and parents, all of whom looked far more severe. The furniture, a mix of stiff-backed chairs and sofas made of glossy fabric, did not seem inviting, and instead gave off a do-not-touch vibe, much like items displayed at a museum.

"Is this your house?" Adam couldn't help asking.

The little girl nodded, looking rather unimpressed by the magnificence around her.

"Who are you?" asked Adam.

The little girl gave him a weird look as she led him through the foyer. "You know who I am."

"No, I don't."

"Yes, you do."

Something odd was going on. Adam debated leaving, but then he smelled the delicious aroma of cooked chicken. His mouth watered. It had been close to dinnertime when he left home, but the sun here had been almost directly overhead. It must be lunchtime, then.

"Mommy, Daddy!" the girl called. "Adam is here."

Adam blinked. "How do you know my name?"

Before the girl could answer, a frowning couple emerged from one of the doorways. They were the same people he'd seen in the portraits, and they were stylishly dressed in nice, if old-fashioned, clothes. The man rubbed his sallow face and eyed Adam with distaste. Next to him, the woman looked down at Adam as if he were something rotten on the heel of her shoe.

"I've heard about you," the man said without a trace of friendliness. "Just so you know, we keep the business strictly within the bloodline. If this is some ruse to get part of the fortune, you can forget it."

"I—" stammered Adam, "I d-don't know what you mean—"

"It's okay, Daddy, Adam is my friend," the little girl said calmly. "He isn't here for the fortune. He's here for lunch."

Adam thought the man looked somewhat familiar, though he didn't know why. He eyed the three people, not sure whether to make a run for it. He glanced at the snow globe in his hand, which still showed the hillside town. He gave it a quick shake. The snowflakes twirled, but nothing else happened.

He stared at the confetti lying on the bottom of the glass. What if he got stuck there forever, with no way to get back to his own time?

After a tense moment of silence, the mother said testily, "Very well, the more the merrier." She said it with the same enthusiasm as someone being asked to swallow a live spider.

The little girl beamed. Despite Adam's protests, she urged him into the dining room. Plates of hot bread rolls, macaroni-and-tuna salad, and bowls of chicken soup awaited the family on a long rectangular table that could seat ten. Unlit candles rested in the chandelier holders. The green-and-white stripes looked strikingly familiar.

A chubby boy in a velvet suit was already seated at the table and messily gorging on his plate of macaroni salad. The parents sat down at one end of the long table, and the little girl sat down at the other end, as far away from the rest of the family as possible. Adam followed her.

"Look, this is all really nice, but I'm not hungry," he said as his stomach let out a loud rumble.

The girl grinned and passed a bowl of soup to him.

"No thanks," Adam tried again, lowering his voice. "I don't even know who you are."

At this, the little girl crossed her arms. "You have a bad memory." Then she sighed and held out her hand. "Very well, then. My name is Daisy."

"Could've guessed that," Adam mumbled, glancing at the same flower in her hair. He shook her hand. "I'm Adam. But you knew that already."

"I did know. I don't forget things like you do."

Adam blinked at the girl as he remembered something. *Daisy.* It couldn't be the same person, could it?

"Do you know a girl named Francine?" he asked.

"Who?"

"Curly hair, dark skin, lives in New York City . . . ?"

Adam stopped talking when he caught the girl's parents listening with suspicion. He decided to figure it out later. He knew there was a logical reason for all of this. And he supposed a *small* bite of lunch wouldn't hurt in the meantime.

He reluctantly settled into his chair. He picked up the gleaming silver spoon and carefully sipped his soup. His eyes widened. It was extraordinary, unlike any other chicken soup he'd tasted.

Daisy was studying her bowl thoughtfully. "Grandmother taught me how to make this," she said. "I think I did rather well."

Adam gaped at her, unsure if he heard correctly. "*You* made the soup?"

Daisy nodded. "And the macaroni salad, too. The cook helped me." Seeing the look on Adam's face, she explained, "I like to make food. It's fun."

"Wow. How old are you?"

"I'm five."

"I keep telling her we have maids for that," the girl's father said from down the table, sounding unimpressed. "We own the entire town. We don't have to lift a *pinky* if we don't want to. She should be more like her brother, who demands proper respect. Isn't that right, Robbie?"

The chubby boy let out a loud belch, said, "It could use more salt," and scarfed down his third bowl of soup since they'd sat down.

Throughout lunch, the mother asked Adam to remind her who he was again, and how old he was, and what his parents did for a living—the type of steady questions adults ask when they're trying to probe. Because of the long table, Adam had to raise his voice and practically shout, something he wasn't used to. He answered as vaguely as he could, and left out the part about the magic snow globe.

"New York City?" repeated the mother. "That's quite a ways from here."

"He must've taken the train in," said the father to the mother. "Shame, it used to be a mighty respectable way to travel, but any riffraff can ride them nowadays." He added, "Can't trust New Yorkers. Ask if he's in cahoots

with whatshisname and that ridiculous group of vaga-
bonds that came by here the other day. They—"

"I'm sure he isn't. He is much too young."

Adam was indignant at this remark. Whatever they
were talking about, twelve years old was certainly not
too young.

"*Ask* him," retorted the father. "I wouldn't be surprised if that crackpot magician's recruiting children
now, trying to claim our fortune."

"Now, see here, Robert . . ."

As the parents continued arguing, Adam leaned
closer to Daisy and murmured, so the others wouldn't
hear, "How did you know I'd be in the garden?"

"Last time you saw me, you said you'd arrive again
on the fourth Monday of May at eleven o'clock," the girl
replied. "And here you are."

"But I've never met you before," Adam insisted.
"*When* did I meet you?"

"A month ago, not long after Grandmother's funeral."

"Impossible."

"You're just like Mommy. She has a bad memory too.
One time she ate breakfast twice, because she forgot she
already ate that morning. Another time she went outside
in the rain without her umbrella, came back to get it, and
forgot it again."

Adam glanced at the arguing adults, then asked
Daisy, "So you don't know anyone from New York City
named Francine?"

Daisy shook her head. "I've never been to the city. Mommy says it's not safe."

Daisy's parents finally ended their argument, and Daisy's mother joined in Adam and Daisy's conversation. "Yes, too many jealous folks in that city. They say the nastiest things to us, thanks to that ex-magician spreading rumors. Ever since he got out of jail—"

Daisy's father snorted. "That's what you get when you're a successful multimillionaire," he gloated, and leaned forward to get another helping of salad. As he did, Adam caught sight of a golden pendulum glistening underneath his collar.

The Gold Mold! Adam thought, recalling what Jack had told him. With a jolt, he recognized the man sitting across the table.

"You—you're Robert Baron!" he gasped, remembering the newspaper clippings.

"*The* Robert Baron is my father," the man said haughtily. "I am Robert Baron the Second. And this is Robert Baron the Third," he added, motioning proudly to the chubby boy down the table.

"What—what year is it?" asked Adam.

Asking someone what year it is, of course, is as common as asking how many potatoes they have in their pocket. After a long, awkward pause, Daisy's mother crinkled her eyebrows and said, "Well, it's been 1922 for five months, hasn't it?"

It all made sense now. Adam was in the Baron

household, the owners of Candlewick's Candles Corporation. He began breathing heavily, the way he did after an intense run in gym class.

Meanwhile, the rest of the family was oblivious to how Adam had gone pale. Mrs. Baron excused herself and disappeared to another room with her half-full plate. Her son, who would one day become the *actual* Gold Mold, was now concentrating on a roll. His father, Robert Baron II, was boasting about his state-of-the-art electric dishwasher.

"I can get the latest technology—the best telephone sets and radios," he was saying. "In fact, I can get anything I want. If I want ice-cold lemon sherbet right now, I have someone who will pick it up for me from the finest dessert shop in the New York area. If I desire a brand-new Rolls-Royce—the finest automobile around—I can have it tomorrow. I can even get another pesky cat for Daisy to replace Mr. Flabbypaws."

Daisy shook her head. "No one can replace Dr. Tabbypaws," she said sadly. Seeing Adam's confused look, she proceeded to describe the daily activities of Dr. Tabbypaws, her strange orange cat who did not like Daisy's father and often hid his shoes and cigars in the litter box. Adam thought the cat was quite clever not to like Robert Baron II.

"I used to have a pet mouse," said Adam, recovering from his initial shock. "It slept under my bed."

"Dr. Tabbypaws used to sleep under my bed,"

said Daisy. "Now he's pushing daisies in the ground." She giggled at the phrase, then looked at Adam and explained, "That's a euphemism. It's a politer way of saying someone died."

Adam was taken aback. The little girl acted much older than five. "Sorry about your cat," he murmured. Then, after a brief pause, he said, "Listen, speaking of death . . ." He tried to think of a good way to bring up the impending fire—one that wouldn't happen for over forty years, but which would nonetheless kill one member at the table.

"It's inevitable," Daisy answered before Adam got a chance to continue.

"What?"

"Death. It's inevitable. That's another word Grandmother taught me. It means 'bound to happen.' Just like how my flowers always die in autumn." The little girl nodded to the window, where they could glimpse the garden. "But then new seeds will grow, and the cycle repeats itself, like the seasons do."

Adam stared at the five-year-old, who he decided was indeed far more mature and intelligent than half his classmates.

"I don't mean to interrupt," interrupted Robert Baron II sarcastically from the other end of the table, "but nobody wants to discuss gardening over lunch. Why don't we talk about something more appropriate, like money? How much money do your folks make, Adam?"

Luckily, before Adam could answer, Robert Baron III reached over for more soup and knocked over three empty dishes with his large belly. His father sighed impatiently, then clutched the pendulum around his neck and yelled for the maids.

Adam suddenly felt drawn to help pick up the dishes, too. Not only that, but he felt compelled to help Robert Baron II with whatever demands the man needed, even if it was something as farfetched as climbing the tallest oak tree to retrieve its highest acorn. He rose from his seat in a dreamlike quality.

"Not *you*," the elder Robert Baron barked at his son, who had also risen halfway to help clean up the mess. Quick as a blink, Adam's mind began returning to normal—though parts of it remained curiously blank. He felt as if he'd just broken the surface of a pool of water after holding his breath underneath for several long moments. For a while longer, he forgot what was going on around him and stood still while a group of maids fervently swept up the mess.

After the mess was cleared, Daisy's father left the room mumbling about pesky children. As Adam finally and fully regained his senses, a question popped into his head. He turned to Daisy and asked, "Does your dad use the pendulum to—to—*hypnotize* people?"

Daisy bit her lip and didn't answer.

"He doesn't hypnotize you, right?" Adam pressed. "You aren't forced to cook for him?"

At this, Daisy laughed. "No, I really do enjoy making food," she reassured him. "Especially sweets. I've been testing flavors since I last saw you. I'm leaning toward cream, with a hint of strawberry and lemon. I think they'd be lovely to share with friends—"

"You don't have any friends," sneered her brother. "Besides, who needs to make candies when you can just *buy* them?" He let out another belch, then waddled out of the room.

Adam thought of the Bittersweet Bonbons from Francine, as well as Jack's story about the Gold Mold's rivalry, and once again wondered if this Daisy was the same candy maker. He was about to mention this, when Daisy said to him, "I'm going to help bring the dishes back to the kitchen. You should go. Your snow globe is empty again."

Adam glanced at the snow globe on the table, which he had almost forgotten. The town inside had vanished.

"How did you know—?" he began.

"It was really kind of you to join us, just like you promised," Daisy said, her eyes bright. "You weren't lying about what you told me last time either, then? That you've tried my candies and love them?"

"Well—I've tried a couple, I think," said Adam hesitantly. "Someone did tell me you're the best candy maker in all of New York."

Daisy nodded. She headed for the doorway with a

determined look, a trace of a smile on her face. "Till next time," was all she said before leaving the room.

Confused, Adam picked up the snow globe and watched the snow confetti twirl.

A split second later, he was back in his bedroom. The dining room, the silverware and dishes, the mansion had all vanished. Downstairs, Uncle Henry was calling him to dinner.

The next day after school, the first thing Adam did was hike to the library. He knew he should get home—the Biscuit Basket was likely already swamped—but something had occurred to him that morning while his science teacher expounded upon the brief existence of the mayfly. "Think of *that* obituary," Ms. Thyme had said. "An entire life cycle, all lived in a day!"

When he walked inside, Adam did not make his customary beeline to the local archives, which contained the collection about Candlewick's Candles Corporation.

Instead, he pored over microfilms of death notices in the region from August 1967.

After an hour of squinting at tiny print, he finally found what he'd been looking for.

Candlewick, N.Y. – Robert Tweed Baron III, 53, died Tuesday, August 15, 1967, in the tragic fire that engulfed the factory headquarters of Candlewick's Candles Corporation.

Born and raised in Candlewick, Baron inherited the famed candle factory from his father, Robert Tweed Baron II, and oversaw its continued success until disaster struck earlier this month.

Mr. Baron will be remembered for his lifelong devotion to wealth accrual and meticulous maintenance of his cigar collection. He is survived by his sister, Daisy Aster Baron, a New York City–based confectioner, and his son, Robert Tweed Baron IV, whose current whereabouts are unknown.

CHAPTER THIRTEEN

THE TIME TOUCH

The rise and demise of Elbert the Excellent was popular gossip in the streets of New York City. Almost everyone knew about his short stint in jail, and in the years that followed, those who encountered him noted how he never was the same afterward. People glimpsed him standing alone in odd places, like a churchyard cemetery in the middle of the night, or an abandoned theater stage at dawn.

Soon, he was nicknamed Elbert the Eccentric. There were whispers about his travels outside of New York with a secretive group of people. Witnesses reported seeing him as far away as London. "Saw him at some clock tower," one person insisted. "Just stood there for eight hours straight, asking passersby for details about some fellow who worked there ages ago. Pretty unusual stuff, if you ask me."

Elbert ignored what people were saying about him.

His life had been shaken, and his mission to acquire and wield the power of the mysterious time touch was more important than ever now. He called together some of his most devoted fans, the same ones who had supported him in his magician days and who had spread the word of his candles. They were delighted to assist their favorite magician on his legendary quest. Together with this group of protégés, he traveled the world, seeking the last piece of the time touch: the one he hoped could reverse the past.

If Elbert had found Santiago irritatingly cryptic, his close group of followers soon found Elbert even more so. Elbert had a penchant for enigmatic sentences and puzzling phrases. He often referred to the treasure they sought as "the one in which past days unfold."

"The treasure we seek is more powerful than anything the world has ever seen," he told his followers. "It's an ancient magic. You'll recognize it if you find it."

In another instance, he explained the treasure as an object containing the fabric of time itself. "Quite dangerous, as the powers can manifest for the worse, if the owner isn't careful."

One of the places he and his followers occasionally frequented was a small town by the name of Candlewick. He'd stare at the candlelit lampposts on the streets, muttering under his breath. Often, he was seen flitting about the town's newly famous candle factory, where he looked in the windows every chance he got, or else near a large mansion up the hill. He was careful to evade authorities each time the owners of the mansion complained.

A passerby in town asked him one day what he was up to, after witnessing Elbert cursing at a lamppost.

"Well, you see, I've been the biggest fool on this side of the ocean," Elbert replied calmly to the baffled passerby. "He's been using my pendulum. I've seen glimpses of him with it. That's how he gets away with his many atrocious misdeeds. And that's another thing he stole from me—from Santiago." He looked down the hill in the direction of the candle factory. A dark shadow passed briefly across his face, then was replaced by his calm smile again. "We need to find the last one. The one that can reverse all this. We *must* find it."

The passerby merely nodded as if he understood. It seemed safer to pretend to agree.

"It took me a while to realize just how he managed such great success in so little time," Elbert continued conversationally. "But it all makes perfect sense now. What he took from me, it was more powerful than I'd realized. Tell me, which worries you more, sir? The past or the future?"

"Neither. I'm more concerned with today."

Elbert smiled. "Then you are better than most people. Tell me this then, sir, when you focus on today's troubles, your mind thinks of little else, correct?"

"I don't know about that."

"Sure you do," insisted Elbert, his smile growing until he was grinning crookedly ear-to-ear. "Try to think about what you're having for dinner tonight and, at the same time, try to think about how much a pinstripe hat costs. You'll find that it's impossible to think two thoughts at once."

"Sure, but I can think of them one after the other."

"However, you can't think of them at the *exact* same time."

"I suppose not," the passerby agreed.

"I'll let you in on a little secret. That is the key to hypnotism. Existing in the absolute present, right down to each second, and bringing someone else into that golden space with you." Elbert looked into the distance, toward the mansion up the hill. "'The one in which lie gifts of gold.' Of course, the physical gold isn't what's important. The gift, the *present*, lies within. The only problem is, if it truly contains the time touch, it's extremely dangerous. It could lead to disastrous effects, I imagine. Because, let me ask you this, what if you were forced to spend most of your day thinking of one thing, and nothing else? What if, against your will, you think only of pinstripe hats for multiple days? Weeks? Everything else will escape your notice. You'll forget who you are—unless you're a pinstripe hat yourself. Do you know what I mean?"

The passerby shook his head, then quickly walked away.

"Shame he went off the deep end," the passerby later said as he retold the story to an interested crowd. "He used to be quite brilliant."

CHAPTER FOURTEEN

RULES OF TRAVEL

A few days after Adam visited the Barons in the 1920s, before he had time to fully comprehend that day's bizarre events, the snow globe changed again. The cemetery was back in the glass, and stayed that way the entire night.

This time, Adam resolved to take the journey, despite the fear of whatever he might find on the other end. He still didn't like the idea of traveling to a cemetery—especially after all he'd learned—but he was determined to understand the snow globe. After making sure Uncle Henry had fallen asleep, he quietly got dressed. With slightly trembling hands, he gave the snow globe a gentle shake.

His bedroom was replaced by a vast field of graves, with thick black woods clustered at the edges. The sky was as white as the mist that rolled across the deserted cemetery. Marble angels guarded the headstones. In the fog, their silhouettes made them seem real, their wings poised to fly to the heavens. Adam had to rub his eyes to make sure he was seeing correctly.

The entrance to the cemetery stood next to Adam, a stone arch towering above wrought iron gates. CANDLE-WICK CEMETERY, it announced. Engraved underneath was an inscription: BLESSED ARE THOSE WHO MOURN, FOR THEY WILL BE COMFORTED.

Adam slowly went into the cemetery, his shoes shuffling along the dewy grass. The cloudy day, the gravestones, the eerie quietness of it all gave him the shivers. They also reminded him of a similar day seven years ago, though that had been at a different cemetery. He recalled again the crows, the two black caskets that lay side by side, the bundles of white flowers. He recalled the adults in pressed collared shirts who told Adam that they were terribly sorry for his loss.

Adam circled the gravestones, half-afraid to read them. But he didn't recognize any of the names.

The edge of the cemetery revealed another level beneath the hill. He peered down into the mist. There, to his surprise, he spotted a boy in an aviator helmet standing beside one of the graves. A bicycle lay next to him in the grass.

"Jack?" Adam called out timidly. He headed down the slope.

Jack looked as startled as Adam felt. For a moment, neither of them said anything.

"I knew you'd be back," Jack finally said with a grin. His eyes lingered on Adam's winter coat. "A bit warm for that, isn't it?"

Adam didn't know what to say. He wasn't quite sure what year it was, let alone the month.

Jack went back to looking at the gravestone beside him. Adam glanced at the inscription.

HERE LIES ELBERT WALSH
DEC 5, 1890 – JUN 1, 1960
Candle Maker Extraordinaire
Who Discovered the True Gifts of Gold

"My grandpa," Jack explained shortly. "He was a magician."

"I'm sorry," Adam murmured. He had never really known his own grandparents, on either side of his family.

"It was a while ago. I was pretty young." Jack looked back at the gravestone. "But I still remember him. He traveled all over the world—Grandma Angie and Dad used to tell me all these fantastic stories about him. So . . . I like to visit, and imagine asking him questions about his travels."

Adam thought of something. "What's today's date?" he asked.

Jack answered it was the thirteenth of August. That explained the warm weather.

"No, I meant . . ." Adam wanted to ask what year

it was, but paused. He didn't want Jack to know he was from the future. At least, not yet.

While Adam debated what to say, Jack gave him a wary look. When Adam didn't say anything, Jack murmured, "Grandpa would never have wanted to be buried here. But Dad said it was the easiest thing to do." He spoke with a faraway look in his eyes, as if he were talking to the trees in the distance. Then he bent down and adjusted a small compass that had been perched against the headstone. A note tucked under the compass read:

STILL SEARCHING FOR THE ONE
TO TURN BACK TIME
—Claudia and your faithful comrades

"His friends still come by to pay their respects," Jack said. "They were all really nice to me, even though my dad thought they were a little off. They had these fantastical ideas about time and magic. Dad told me Grandpa's priorities had changed by the time he was born, and his days of journeying with his group were over, but . . ." Jack glanced at the card again. "Seems they'll always continue in his footsteps and keep sharing his ideas."

Adam was intrigued. "What kind of ideas?"

Jack blinked and seemed surprised Adam had asked. "Nothing. Kind of complicated to get into." Then he said abruptly, "I'm going to the city. Want to come?"

With that, Jack hopped on his bike and pedaled toward the cemetery entrance, leaving Adam behind. Stunned, Adam glanced at his snow globe. The tiny cemetery was still inside. He shook it. Nothing happened.

He did the only thing he could think of. He ran after Jack, yelling, "Wait up!"

He passed the cluster of woods. The black trees stood idly against the white haze, their skeletal branches both enchanting and sinister. Over the treetops, Adam glimpsed the topmost part of a familiar smokestack. He realized the town of Candlewick must be on the other side.

Down the path was a deserted train station. Jack had stopped beside a bench on the platform, huffing for air. He adjusted his aviator helmet. Adam caught up to him.

"Hey . . . did you ever get my music box?" Jack asked when his breathing slowed.

"Huh?"

"I went back to my old place before coming to the cemetery, and the music box was gone," Jack went on. "I was hoping . . ." Jack saw the confused look on Adam's face, then looked away. "Never mind. For some reason I thought you'd have it."

Adam swallowed and said carefully, "I'm sorry. I don't know what you're talking about."

Jack didn't reply. Instead, he busied himself with locking his bicycle to the bench. Adam tried to think of something to say but couldn't. He didn't think now was a good time to bring up the factory fire.

A few minutes later, a sleek black train arrived. Jack hopped aboard, and Adam hesitantly followed suit. They went down the train corridor and found an empty compartment. It was surprisingly nice and spacious.

Adam didn't have a train ticket, and he murmured this worry as he sat down on the brown leather seat across from Jack.

"Don't worry about it," Jack reassured him. "It's a short ride. They won't check."

He tugged on his aviator helmet and looked out the window. They rode in silence. Adam was too busy worrying about whether he'd get thrown in jail to admire the view of the countryside as the train rolled past, but luckily no one stopped by their compartment. The skyline of Manhattan approached in the distance. A few stops later, they arrived at Grand Central Station.

Jack jumped through the exit, ducking past an approaching conductor collecting tickets and prompting an angry shout from the man. Adam used this opportunity to slip past as well, clutching the snow globe tightly under his arm.

Adam had been through the station many times in his life. Even thirty years ago, the station was a gem of a building, with enormous windows and wide marble columns. But the building was showing signs of age, and Adam allowed himself a rare smile, knowing that back in his own time, a massive restoration project had just been completed that made the station sparkle like new. Until that moment, he'd never fully considered the hundreds of thousands of people the train station had seen—not just in his own years, but in decades past.

Outside on 42nd Street, Adam saw immediately that the city had changed from when he'd visited in the 1930s, in the sense that there were more modern-looking pay phones, faster and sleeker cars, and heavy color televisions blaring in window displays. People wore slightly longer coats and larger glasses, and the women had larger hairdos that covered their foreheads. There was new technology being boasted in stores. Adam stared for a few seconds at a shiny turquoise contraption in a store window before realizing it was a toaster.

People still hurried down the streets with the familiar sense of haste common to the city, passing by notices here and there that warned the public against "the Reds."

"Who are the Reds?" Adam asked Jack.

Jack looked at him strangely. "Do you live under a rock? The Reds are Communists. The United States is at war against them."

Probably because he realized Adam was still confused, Jack explained as they walked. He likened the war to a game of chess in which a white team and a red team try to wipe each other out and take over the chessboard. The trouble was, each team had equal amounts of brilliant and stubborn players, and it was nearly impossible to win.

"So the red team are the bad guys?" asked Adam.

"Yes," said Jack, and then he laughed. "Although I suppose they think *we're* the bad guys."

Adam was glad to see Jack smile. But he knew he had to warn Jack about the factory fire soon. The last time he met Jack was in 1967, the exact month and year of the fire. There might only be mere days before the fire. "Listen, Jack, I have to tell you something—"

"We're here!" Jack interrupted excitedly. They were standing in front of a Midtown movie theater. Jack motioned for Adam to follow, and the pair went inside. Jack snuck a handful of buttery popcorn from an unattended popcorn cart nearby. On the walls were posters advertising the latest movies, including *2001: A Space Odyssey*, which Adam had seen at school on an old sci-fi channel once when they had an enthusiastic substitute teacher.

Jack glanced at the poster and remarked, "I can't wait for the future. You've heard about how they're trying to fly people to the moon, haven't you? Imagine a space mission all the way to Jupiter." He tugged on his aviator helmet and watched Adam closely with an almost knowing look. "How neat is that? I can't *wait* for the new century."

Adam didn't mention that he was only two years away from 2001 back home, and it wasn't anything like the movie yet.

They managed to sneak into one of the showings and

glimpse five minutes of a cowboy film set in the Wild West before the movie manager kicked them out. They ran out of the building into the daylight. Even though Adam was normally not a rule breaker and was silently panicking the entire time they were inside the theater, he found himself grinning. They laughed as they hurried down the streets. The sun had come out from behind the clouds and pleasantly warmed their faces.

Jack pointed to a newsstand. "Want some snacks?"

They went up to a seedy-looking newsstand. Rows of magazines, candy cartons, and newspapers crowded the shelves. To the side sat a small pretzel cart. Hunched inside the newsstand, manning both kiosks, was a bald man in a black leather jacket. An eye patch covered half his face, while a pink scar snaked around the other half. Adam guessed he was about thirty years old, though it was hard to tell with grown-ups. The man chewed on a cigar, absorbed in the comics section of the newspaper, chuckling in a low growl every now and then.

"Hi, Charlie," Jack said to the man.

"Jack," the man said gruffly.

"I'll take two pretzels with mustard, please." Jack held out his empty hand expectantly.

"What, you think I just give away free grub?"

The man and Jack engaged in a glaring contest. Adam took a step backward, his eyes on the vendor's bulging muscles behind the leather sleeves. Was Jack out of his mind?

"You're gonna run me outta business," the man growled after a few seconds, but he retrieved two soft pretzels from the cart. Jack smiled and handed one to Adam.

"How'd you do that?" Adam asked.

The seller waved a hand and said, "Jack's an insider."

"I helped Charlie scare away some kids who kept vandalizing his newsstand last month," Jack explained. "Now he owes me a lifetime supply of pretzels and candy."

It was a good pretzel—soft and salty, with a generous line of mustard along the top. Mustard always made Adam's lips burn, but he loved it nonetheless. He thought of Francine and how she and her friends would share mustard-laden pretzels on their birthdays. How peculiar that they could've done the exact same thing, in the exact same city, decades apart.

Jack finished his in four bites. "Best pretzel in the whole city," he said with his mouth full.

"My uncle makes good pretzels," said Adam. "He runs a bakery."

"What's it called?"

"The Biscuit Basket," said Adam before he caught himself. He added, "It's not going to be open for, uh, a while."

Jack found this oddly funny and snorted in laughter. He helped himself to a piece of bubble gum from the newsstand, which made Charlie snarl, "Shouldn't you be in school? It's Tuesday."

Jack admitted he was skipping class.

"Ya gotta stop this, Jack," replied Charlie.

"Won't your dad be mad?" chimed in Adam.

Jack gave him a hard look. "My dad's gone."

"What are you talking about?"

"What are *you* talking about? He died in the factory fire. I live with my aunt and uncle now, a few towns over."

Adam backtracked. "The . . . fire?"

Jack chewed on the bubble gum, looking disappointed. "You really aren't from the future then, are you?"

Charlie gave the boys an odd look as Adam felt himself turn pale. "Why would you say that?" Adam asked.

Jack looked away. "Just an observation."

Adam swallowed hard. "You—you told me at the cemetery that your grandpa and his friends had fantastical ideas about time and magic . . ."

"Yeah. My grandpa used to study the properties of time." Jack stopped chewing the gum as his expression grew serious. "His friends—followers—once told me there's a high probability that time traveling exists, and that I should watch for signs. For strange events. People showing up and then disappearing, for instance." Jack looked pointedly at Adam. "I've always been keeping a lookout for that kind of thing. But I didn't believe them, not completely. Because if time traveling exists, why do bad things still happen? Shouldn't someone be warning us each time disaster's going to strike?"

"There'd be too many to keep track of," grunted Charlie.

Adam said nothing. It was the very question he'd been wondering too. He held his snow globe tighter and glanced at the newspaper stand. The print date on the front page of the papers read:

AUGUST 13, 1968

Nearly a year after the candle factory burned down.

No wonder Jack seemed a little different from the first time Adam had met him. Adam had dealt with his own loss by retreating into a shell; Jack, by skipping school and acting out.

Charlie helped himself to one of his own pretzels and growled, "Your grandpa sounds like he had some interesting ideas, Jack."

Jack shrugged. "He and his friends believed there are three pieces of time on earth—past, present, and future. And that there's a way to control them." He stopped talking after noticing Adam's expression. "You okay?"

"How?" asked Adam, who was only half listening. His mind was still on the factory. *It burned down a year ago.*

"He said that long ago, the pieces were trapped in containers. If you were lucky enough to find one of them, you could use it to unleash that piece of time's power." Jack shook his head. "A lot of people thought my grandpa was cuckoo. Even my dad didn't listen to him. They called him Elbert the Eccentric." Jack's grin faded as he kicked at the sidewalk. "At least he got a proper burial. The people who died at the factory . . . that was their grave. My dad included."

"Candlewick's Candles," Charlie said with a sigh. "Horrible accident. Story made it to all the papers here. Can't imagine the nightmare those workers went through. All those safety violations they found afterward . . . How'd the owner get away with all that?"

"I think he was controlling them," answered Jack. "That's my guess."

Adam suddenly felt lightheaded, the way he did when a teacher called on him and he had to speak in front of the whole class.

"He was," he said hoarsely.

"What?" asked Jack.

"Robert Baron the Third. The Gold Mold. He used his pendulum to hypnotize people. I mean, his father did, but I'm sure he did too."

"You—you met my dad's boss?"

Adam didn't answer. He didn't understand why the snow globe had brought him to this place, one year after the factory fire. How could he warn Jack now, after the fire had already happened? Nor did he understand why he met the Barons forty-five years before the fire. The visits must be connected, yet the connection wasn't clear.

"Charlie, you got any water back there?" said Jack. "Adam looks like he's about to pass out."

Adam heard Charlie mutter something about annoying kids driving him out of business, which made Jack laugh and say, "Charlie, you'll be here forever."

Charlie rolled his eyes. "Probably." He gave Adam a look of concern before disappearing to rummage behind the window. Jack stood on his tiptoes and leaned over the sill to help.

Meanwhile, Adam started to put down the snow globe and half-eaten pretzel so he could rub his eyes. As he did so, the snow globe tilted, and the snowflake confetti whirled inside the glass.

"Wait!" he shouted, realizing too late that the cemetery inside the glass had disappeared.

The next moment, he was standing in his bedroom again.

He kept shaking the snow globe. "Take me back!" he cried in exasperation.

His exclamation woke his uncle. "Adam?" called Uncle Henry in a groggy voice from the living room. "What's going on?"

Adam noticed the time on his bedside clock. It was almost midnight, the same time he had left.

"Nothing," he answered. "Just a bad dream is all."

On Friday after school, Adam headed for the subway.

Ever since Adam moved to his uncle's place from the

suburbs after his parents died, Uncle Henry had reminded him about the rules of traveling alone in the city:

1. Say where you're going and when you'll be home.
2. Don't talk to strangers.
3. If you ever feel unsafe, go into the nearest store and find a trusted adult.
4. Avoid unlit areas.

Now that Adam was twelve (a perfectly adequate age, despite what Daisy's mother thought), he was venturing to more places on his own, though Uncle Henry preferred him to stay within twenty blocks of home. Anywhere north of Times Square or across a river still worried his uncle, as it was "too far." So Adam hadn't bothered much with going anywhere on the subway—until now.

He'd been working up the courage for a few days and was now determined to find Charlie. The vendor was the one person who could tell him where he might be able to find Jack. And if he found Jack, maybe he could learn more about the fire and Jack's grandfather's theories about time. Adam had memorized the Midtown cross streets where the vendor's newsstand had been situated: 57th and 6th Avenue, not far from Central Park. He could only hope it was still there. He knew that thirty-one years had passed, and the probability was slim, almost impossible. But then again, many impossible things had happened in the past week.

As Adam squeezed past legs and ducked under arms inside the train car, he decided his uncle had forgotten to mention one more rule.

5. Avoid the subway during rush hour, or else you'll get squished like a sandwich.

Adam spent twenty minutes being shoved and jostled before he finally reached his stop. He hurried outside and gulped in the fresh, early evening air. Then he headed down the street where Charlie's newsstand had been thirty-one years ago.

To his great surprise—or, rather, he wasn't *too* surprised, because nothing was surprising these days anymore—the newsstand was still there. And sure enough, hunched behind the window was Charlie, eye patch and cigar and all, looking three decades older. This time, the bald vendor wore a gray windbreaker instead of a leather jacket, and deep lines creased his forehead as he read the newspaper.

Adam timidly approached the man. He had to clear his throat and say hello several times before Charlie heard him.

"Speak up, will ya?" Charlie put down the newspaper and peered over the window. "Whaddya want?"

"You're—you're Charlie, right?" Adam explained

how he was looking for someone who'd visited Charlie's newsstand as a kid. "It's this boy, Jack. He wore an aviator helmet. You knew him thirty-one years ago . . ." He trailed off after seeing no change in Charlie's clueless look.

Charlie squinted his one eye. "What's your name again?"

"I'm . . . um . . . you don't know me."

Charlie suddenly let out a shout of recognition. "You're that kid who disappeared into thin air!"

Several passersby glanced back at the exclamation. Adam stuffed his fists into his jacket, embarrassed.

Charlie had turned pale. His cigar dropped out of his mouth. "I *remember* you," he said shakily. "Scared the living daylights out of me and your friend after you pulled that magic act. My wife wouldn't believe me when I told her. Thought I was tryin' to be funny. You some sort of ghost, boy?"

Adam shook his head. "So do you remember Jack?"

"That was a long time ago. Haven't seen ol' Jack in ages."

Adam's heart fell. "Thank you anyway."

Back at the newsstand, Charlie scratched his head. How odd that the vanishing boy had appeared at his newsstand after so many years. The boy didn't look any older either, if his memory was correct. Then again, most kids looked the same to the vendor: delinquents who wrecked his property and swiped candy and magazines.

Charlie chewed on his cigar. He probably should've told the boy about the stranger who had approached the newsstand a few months ago. The street vendor vividly remembered the man. An uneasy feeling crept up his neck even as he recalled the incident.

The stranger had worn a black suit and had two sharp eyebrows and a pointy chin. He'd arrived at the counter early one morning in late July, clutching a spiral notepad in his long fingers. Charlie remembered thinking the stranger probably needed to see a doctor—he had sickly pale skin, paler than any he'd seen, and a sort of crazed look in his black eyes.

"Are you Charlie?" the stranger had hissed softly.

"Yep. What can I get for ya?"

The stranger flipped to a page in his notepad. "In August of 1968, you and another eyewitness saw a boy vanish into thin air from this very spot. Is this correct?"

Charlie had to consider this for a few moments before he remembered. "Oh, yeah. Thought I imagined it. Scared the heck out of me. Probably a kid magician."

The stranger's dark eyes had glinted in the sunlight. "What was his name?"

"How should I know? I ain't the kid's babysitter."

"Can you describe the boy? Dark hair, gray eyes, short, perhaps?"

"You're asking me about some random kid I met *thirty-one* years ago?"

"Not every kid vanishes into thin air," replied the stranger pointedly.

"I don't answer questions, I sell stuff."

"I should warn you, it's best to cooperate."

"Who even are you?"

The stranger's thin lips curled into a sneer. "Ah-ah. I'm asking the questions here, and I suggest you answer them. Think of your poor wife."

Charlie stiffened.

"It's not easy for you two to make ends meet, is it?" continued the stranger. "Struggling to retire with barely any savings. Imagine what would happen if you ended up losing this newsstand."

"Are you threatening me?" Charlie demanded, cracking his knuckles. No skinny, pale man in a suit intimidated *him*. But the stranger didn't even flinch.

"Try to remember." The stranger's eyes flicked over the bootlegged CDs on the stand. "Or else I'll let the authorities know about your illegal goods . . ."

Charlie fumed, but the thought of his wife stopped him from climbing over the window to pummel the smirk right off the guy's pointy face.

"All I remember is the kid was small," said Charlie. "Looked eight or nine or so. Might've had dark hair."

"And his home? Where was he from?"

"I assume he's from the city, Your Royal Inquisitor," Charlie growled.

"Try to remember any additional details."

"That's all I got. How about you scram?"

The stranger simply sneered and eyed the CDs again.

Charlie closed his eyes and racked his brain. He could make up something, but he had a feeling the stranger would catch on if he told anything less than the truth. As a matter of fact, he did remember a bit about the boy. As the stranger had pointed out, it wasn't every day that he met someone who vanished into thin air.

"Think the kid mentioned at one point he worked at a bakery or whatnot," the vendor finally said. "The name was funny. Two words, both started with the same letter, if I recall."

"A bakery that had a funny name," spat the stranger, as if Charlie was making fun of him.

"Hey, bud, you should be glad I remembered that much. Now how 'bout you tell me your name?"

"That is none of your concern," the stranger answered before slipping away. In a few seconds, he had disappeared around the corner.

The day after the stranger had shown up, the news-stand had a brand-new sign: NO SOLICITING.

Now Charlie thought about the boy again.

"Eh, it's probably nothing," he muttered, flipping the page in the newspaper. "Lousy New Yorkers."

CHAPTER FIFTEEN

THE MATHEMATICIAN

Adam had guessed the venomous M would return one day. Although he hadn't seen the man in a while—and he continued to keep a close lookout each day, walking to school and back—he was certain they would cross paths again.

He was right.

It didn't happen right away. The core of winter was approaching. Schools closed for Thanksgiving break, and the windows of department stores displayed their arrays of winter hats and wool jackets. Every few days, flurries of fat snowflakes filled the city streets, but they didn't stay on the ground for long. The real snowstorms lurked in the distance, unformed clouds of ice and gloom yet to come.

The candles from Francine had long burned down. Uncle Henry bought new ones, so the Biscuit Basket stood aglow, a warm and welcoming break from the cold for passersby. However, the new candles lacked the distinctive style of Francine's striped ones. What's more, as the saying goes, imitation is the sincerest form of flattery. The bakeries two streets over had also adorned their windows with shining candles. The candy shop around the corner had started producing candle-shaped lollipops. Even the coffee shop took part, and went one step further by placing tiny candles on each of its tables and advertising "romantic candlelit tables for two—perfect for a coffee date!"

Uncle Henry was unfazed. They still had a decent number of customers. The baker offered winter specials on batches of cinnamon buns. "The best cure for a chilly day," he claimed, "is a piping hot cinnamon bun straight from the oven."

He was absolutely right. The cinnamon buns sold out each day.

On Thanksgiving Day, Uncle Henry closed the bakery to have a special meal. Amidst the store's bright candles, he and Adam had baked potatoes, fruit salad, cranberry sauce, and one-third of a whole roasted chicken (the rest was saved for later). It was the best supper Adam had ever eaten. They counted their blessings and marveled how just over a month ago, they had almost been evicted because they'd been short on rent.

Later that night, Adam stopped by the Hole to drop off leftover baked potatoes and fruit salad. The shelter was having its own celebration. The aroma of beef stew embraced Adam when he walked in, and had he not been stuffed to the brim already, his mouth would have watered for a bite.

Victor was eating with a small group of people around a table piled with mashed potatoes, two baskets of bread, and bowls of hot stew. Extra lamps had been set up in the corners, brightening the room with a warm, sunny glow. Today, the inhabitants of the shelter no longer wore troubled expressions, but were laughing and chatting like good friends. Despite their misfortune, in that moment, they were happy. The cheerful sight held Adam in place.

When Victor saw Adam, the old man wheeled across the room to greet him. "Hello, fellow! Wonderful day, isn't it?"

"The best." Adam handed the leftovers to Victor. "I ate so much I might explode."

"That'll be me by the end of tonight. Who knew there are so many foods I'm thankful for?"

Adam watched Victor put the food on the table for the others. A few of the people clapped Victor on the back. Grinning toothlessly, Victor returned to Adam.

"Will you be staying?" he asked.

"No, it's almost bedtime. But thank you." Adam glanced at the group at the table and thought of Francine. "Can I ask you something, Victor?"

"Fire away."

"I was just wondering . . . do these people here have families?"

"The sad truth is, no, not really. A lot of them don't have families or friends to turn to in times of need. But that's what this place is for. Here, we become sort of a temporary family for each other. Even if we don't know everyone's names."

"What about you? You don't have a real family either?"

Victor shook his head. "Not in the sense you mean."

Adam suddenly realized in all these years, he had never asked Victor about his background. He had only heard the old man tell other people's tales, but never his own, aside from the stories about his leg.

"What did you do before you came to the Hole?" Adam asked.

"Hm, interesting question." The old man paused for a few moments. "The story of my past is long and full of twists and turns. It would take twelve months to recount it all." He smiled and peered at Adam. "Come with me. I want to show you something."

Adam had never been past the kitchen before. He followed Victor down a dim corridor, the sound of his footsteps and Victor's wheels muffled against the frayed carpet. Victor paused in front of Door 6, and used his key to unlock the knob. Inside was a cramped room even smaller than Adam's tiny bedroom. It contained only a simple bed and a plastic bin of clothing.

Despite the barren space, it was clear that Victor had tried to spruce it up to make it more homey. Along the tiny windowsill were tiny pieces of dried flowers, arranged by type and color. Pasted to the wall next to the bed were posters of galaxies and solar systems. To Adam's surprise, textbooks sat against the opposite wall. He tilted his head to read the spines. They were heavy textbooks on mathematics and space.

Victor followed Adam's gaze and grinned. "Yes, those are what I wanted to show you," he said. "I need to return them soon. A professor at the university up the street let me borrow them for some light reading."

"*Light* reading?" repeated Adam.

"Well, light to me. At one point in my early life, I was a mathematician."

Now, much like a writer, an actuary, or a professional dog-food taster, a mathematician has one of the most misunderstood jobs in the world. A mathematician's work can be described as one similar to a detective's. Both involve complicated puzzles and mysteries, and people in both professions try to find a logical pattern behind the puzzles. Consider Nicolaus Copernicus, for example, one of the greatest mathematicians in history, who helped prove Earth rotates around the sun, and not the other way around, as millions of people had believed. Or Florence Nightingale, whose mathematical study of hospitals improved their condition and thus kept numerous patients from dying. Throughout time, mathematicians have made possible what was previously thought impossible.

Adam had not thought much about what he'd like to be when he got older. For a brief period, he had wavered between veterinarian and zookeeper. But after listening to Victor explain what a mathematician does, he was convinced his future career was to be a mathematician too. He listened raptly as Victor recounted his university days solving equations and figuring out puzzles.

"I had a very cool idea for a project involving permutations," Victor said.

"What's a permutation?" Adam asked.

"I bet you're familiar with the concept without knowing the word," Victor said kindly. "Imagine you had a spoon, a fork, and a knife. How many ways can you arrange them? First the spoon, then the fork, and last the knife. Or how about, first the knife, then the spoon, and last the fork? Now, imagine you had one thousand spoons, each a slightly different color. What then? Red spoon, fork, blue spoon, green spoon, knife. Or blue spoon, fork, red spoon, green spoon, knife, and so on. You can have a near-infinite amount of combinations, if the set is large and diverse enough. In math, we call these permutations. That is the simplified concept of what was at the heart of my project. But my department ran out of funding before I could really get going on it."

"You had no money?"

"No money," Victor repeated. "My project was stalled. That was the end of my career as a mathematician. In truth, that was the first of a handful of big blows in my life. A slippery slope, from which I found it diffi-cult to recover."

Adam knew what it was like not to have enough money for something he wanted. "That stinks," he mumbled. "If only we could change the past."

"Ah, but it wouldn't be that simple! Part of why I loved that project so much is the concept of infinity. Life is full of infinite possibilities. Many permutations. And once a permutation is set, it connects to the next one, as if on a string. It's all intertwined. The string of my life has taken me places I never imagined, and I am who I am today because of my past."

A former mathematician who's now stuck working in the Hole, thought Adam. He didn't say aloud how dismal that was.

One of Victor's neighbors peeked in the doorway. He nodded at Adam awkwardly and shifted his hands inside his oversized coat. Then he bid Victor to rejoin them at the dinner table.

"There won't be any bread left if you dawdle, brother!"

"Coming," chuckled Victor.

After the man left, Adam asked, "That was your brother?"

"No, we're not related by blood. But he's my brother in every other way. He's a friend. And friends are like family." Victor smiled. "Sorry, but the party's waiting. Don't want all the baguettes to disappear!"

Adam bid goodbye to Victor, then headed home. As soon as the Biscuit Basket came into view, he could tell something was wrong.

Flashing blue-and-red lights of two parked police cars lit up the street. One of the bakery windows was broken. Three of Uncle Henry's cakes on display were overturned. Inside, shattered glass and molten candle wax smeared the bakery floors.

Uncle Henry was in the middle of speaking to two police officers. He saw Adam and waved him inside with a sense of urgency.

"What happened?" Adam asked.

"Vandalism," answered one of the officers. She held up a sharp rock the size of her palm.

Adam stared at the rock, baffled. "Do you know who did it?"

Uncle Henry told the story. He hadn't yet pulled down the metal security screen in front of the bakery, as he'd been in the back room, preparing some dough for the next day, when he'd heard the glass shatter. He dashed out wielding a large rolling pin and found a tall figure, who immediately turned and ran out of the bakery. The cakes and the burning candles had already been knocked over, and Uncle Henry was too busy putting out the flames to chase the perpetrator into the street outside.

"You're lucky this place didn't burn down," said the

other officer. "Candles are dangerous to display in a shop. Huge fire hazards."

"We snuff the candles out every night before bed," Uncle Henry quickly reassured him.

Uncle Henry went to get a broom to sweep up the mess. Meanwhile, the police asked Adam if he saw anyone suspicious on the streets. He hadn't—at least, not in a while. A chilly breeze passed through the hole in the window. Adam shivered, but for a slightly different reason.

"I think I know who it was," he whispered.

He told them his theory that M had returned to the shop, though leaving out the part that M was chasing after a magic snow globe. Unfortunately, without evidence, the police couldn't confirm the culprit was M. Besides, they told Adam, a name like M was not much to go on. But the officers jotted down Adam's description of the man.

When Uncle Henry at last emerged with a broom and dustpan, the police instructed him and Adam to keep vigilant and to call if the perpetrator returned.

After the police left, Adam helped his uncle patch up the window temporarily with cardboard and duct tape. They swept up the broken glass pieces, scraped away the wax, and cleaned up the smashed cakes.

"The bakery will have to remain closed until the window's fixed," said Uncle Henry. He shook his head and muttered, "Why would anyone do this?"

Adam knew why, of course. He swallowed. "Uncle Henry, I have to tell you something."

Adam went upstairs and returned with the snow globe. He told his uncle all about the magic behind the snow globe, about the crazy adventures he'd had, and the people he'd encountered. He told him about meeting Francine the candle seller, and about the town where the candle factory had stood. He told his uncle about Jack and their trip to New York City in 1968. He told him his suspicion that it was M who'd vandalized the bakery that night, in search of the snow globe. Uncle Henry listened quietly and did not interrupt.

Finally, once Adam finished, Uncle Henry said gently, "Your parents were natural explorers, Adam. It wouldn't surprise me if you inherited some of that, and went traveling in your dreams."

Adam's mouth fell open. "These weren't *dreams*! Candlewick is a real town! Or was!"

"I've also traveled to real places in my dreams. You say these travels happen only at night?"

"Not the first time!" said Adam, catching Uncle Henry's knowing eyebrow raise. "That time was in the afternoon."

Even so, he knew the story wasn't convincing. Uncle Henry gave him a worried frown, then placed a hand on his shoulder. "Don't worry about this shady M character.

This mess tonight was probably done by one of the other bakers. They don't like the competition, you know, now that we're getting successful."

"But—"

"It's getting late. You should go to bed. Here, take your snow globe with you."

Adam sucked in his cheeks. There was no use arguing. "Yes, Uncle Henry," he mumbled as he shuffled toward the stairs.

On his way, he passed the patched-up window where, right outside the bakery, on the other side of the wall, lurked a tall man in a black suit.

Uncle Henry was not the only person who had heard Adam's tale about the snow globe.

CHAPTER SIXTEEN

BURNED

The Biscuit Basket remained closed for the next few days. There were a lot of back-and-forth negotiations with the insurance company. The initial cost of repairing the window would take a good chunk of money from Uncle Henry's savings, but thanks to the earnings from the previous month, they wouldn't be scraping for cash.

Adam stayed hunched in his bedroom for most of the weekend, staring at the empty snow globe. The longer the snow globe remained blank, the more miserable he felt. And like the snow globe, he had nothing: no leads on the mysterious M, no proof of the snow globe's magic for the police or his uncle, and no idea what to do.

The unknown tends to scare people because it makes us jump to many different conclusions. If your closet door swings open on its own in the middle of the night, for example, you might think you have a ghost on your hands, when it could just as likely be a faulty latch or a draft. Or if someone suddenly disappears, never to be heard from again, you might think they have been taken by kidnappers or monsters from the lagoon, when it's equally likely they simply decided to go on a long vacation without any of their belongings. But because our minds never truly know the truth in these cases, we can simply go about guessing all day.

For Adam, the two biggest unknowns occupying his mind were: 1) the true extent of his and his uncle's safety, and 2) the likelihood that he'd ever be able to warn the townspeople of Candlewick of the fire before it started.

To say nothing of other past events closer to his heart he'd desperately like to change.

Then, on Sunday evening, it happened. A landscape finally emerged inside the snow globe.

It was Candlewick.

This might be his chance. Adam anxiously waited until Uncle Henry had gone to bed, and, for good measure, sat tight until his uncle's snores in the living room reached a steady rhythm. Then Adam took the snow globe and gave it a small shake.

Snowflake confetti swirled inside the glass. Adam was already thinking about what he'd do once he got to the town. He didn't know how much time he had, so he needed to hurry.

In a blink, Adam was back on the same hillside outside the town of Candlewick. Though the air was warm, the stars winked coldly overhead against the inky sky.

He started toward the town, but by the time he reached the outskirts, he realized something was very, very wrong.

Only a few of the houses had their lights on. Most of the windows along every street were as dark as the streets themselves. Cars had vanished from driveways. None of the lampposts were lit. Worst of all, a stale layer of smoke hung in the air, along with a familiar scorched smell. Adam sniffed the air again. To his horror, he recognized what the smell was: burned candle wax. It was the same smell that had stuck to the floors of his uncle's bakery a few days ago.

He peered desperately into the distance, where the candle factory stood isolated in the dark. Its ominous smokestacks were dormant. None of its windows were lit either. "That doesn't mean anything," Adam told himself. After all, the place was still standing.

Had he been close enough, Adam would have realized each window had been completely shattered.

As Adam stumbled ahead, the smell of smoke grew stronger. He arrived at the first street and slowly passed the houses, looking around for a sign of someone—anyone.

The first few homes were empty. The next house had a dog barking indoors. Adam went up to the window for a closer look. The living room was dark. In the dim moonlight, he could make out the shapes of various pieces of furniture—a sofa, the silhouette of a bookcase.

Remnants of flowers were strewn on the windowsill next to a shallow vase in which very little water remained. A lonely Boston terrier yapped tirelessly at the front door. It raised its white-and-black head and, upon seeing Adam, whimpered through the window.

Adam tried the door handle. Locked.

The dog's owners were not there. Hanging on the wall next to the dog was a photo of a middle-aged couple. Adam had a sinking feeling he knew where they'd gone.

"Poor thing," Adam whispered. The dog reminded him of his own beloved Speedy. The next moment, Adam had gently lifted the window. The terrier leaped outside and bounded into his arms, where he curled into a whimpering ball. The dog gave Adam courage as he kept walking.

Several houses later, Adam came across the first people. A mother and her daughter were packing suitcases into a car in their garage. Adam timidly approached them.

"Excuse me," he said. "Did something happen here?"

The mother turned to him in surprise. Her eyes were puffy and had dark circles underneath. "Why, yes, child. Didn't you hear about the disaster?"

The daughter, a wiry teenager, spoke up. "The factory burned down two weeks ago. A lot of people in town died."

Adam stared at them. No, it was not possible. There was still time, there had to be—

"There's nothing left for us here," said the mother.

She cast a weary glance at their suitcases. "Most of us survivors are leaving town. Without the candle factory, there is no source of income. My husband would—" She gasped with a shudder and hid her face in her sleeve.

"My—my dad was killed in the fire," explained the girl, clearly trying to appear brave, but the flicker of fear and shock in her red-rimmed eyes gave her away. "Where's your family?"

Adam's heart hammered. He had to get to Jack's house. "I'm sorry. I—I have to go. But first—" He held up the whimpering terrier in his arms. "Do you think you could? I found him abandoned."

"Oh, that's the Bordens' old dog," said the mother. "They were both in the middle of their shift when the fire broke out."

"Mom?" said the daughter, after a long pause.

The mother sighed. "Yes, dear, of course we can take him."

After they exchanged goodbyes, Adam turned and started running. He sprinted up and down the next hills, coughing from the smoke.

Across the desolate town, the few folks that Adam ran into were either packing up and leaving or looking lost and scared. An old man stood on his porch silently staring into the distance. Twice, someone asked Adam if he was all right. He answered yes but hurried along. His hasty footsteps disturbed the confetti in his snow globe, but the town inside the glass had not disappeared yet.

When he arrived at the redbrick, two-story house on Oak Street, his stomach sank again. The front porch light was off, like all the others up and down the street. The windows were pitch black. Adam pounded on the door, but no one answered. This door was also locked.

He peered inside Jack's bedroom window. The bedsheets were gone. Half the books and magazines on the bookshelf had disappeared. A few of Jack's model airplanes remained, including the one that was half-finished last time. That particular model had now been completed, and sat in the same spot on the writing desk. Next to it were a few sheets of paper, the candlestick—this time with an unlit, white-and-green-striped candle in it—and, in the corner of the desk, Jack's music box, its lid firmly shut.

Dejected, Adam looked around at the darkening town. Looming ahead of him, much larger now, was the scene of the disaster—Candlewick's Candles Corporation.

He found himself slowly trudging to the factory. He needed to see the destruction with his own eyes. Even though the main walls of the factory remained standing, the inside looked like a demolition site, with its window shards and piles of broken cement and black rubble. There was a stillness in the air, heavy with smoke and the scent of lavender left over from the burned candles.

Adam stood alone in the dark, helplessly rooted to the spot, not wanting to move. When he finally shifted sideways, his foot unearthed a scrap of clothing.

Later, when recounting these dark events, Adam would leave out these details, because he didn't want to admit that he had gotten terribly sick at the sight, and had thrown up like he had the stomach flu. He didn't want to admit how he'd rolled up into a ball, coughing and crying until his eyes were swollen.

When he finally managed to pull himself together, something metallic in the rubble near his feet caught his eye. It glistened in the starlight. Adam carefully dug out the object from beneath the black soot and examined it, but he couldn't make out what it was.

He slipped it into his pocket and wiped some of the grime and tears from his face. Other things were distracting him at the moment—like the fact that he needed to wash up badly. He decided to try Jack's house again.

There was still no answer when he knocked on the door, but the window to Jack's bedroom was unlocked. Adam pushed it upward. "Hello?" he called inside.

Breaking into someone's house, of course, is frowned upon in many places, if not outright against the law. But sometimes there is a dire need to break the rules for a very good reason. For example, using the forbidden back door of the school to get inside, because a pair of sixth-grade bullies awaited you in the front each morning to dunk your head in the toilet. Or skipping homework in order to help your uncle manage the bakery, because otherwise you might not have a roof over your head the next month. In those cases, it is up to you to decide whether to risk one thing for something more catastrophic.

Adam took the chance and heaved himself through the window. Again, it was lucky he was so small. He slid inside easily.

He turned on the light switch. That was when he noticed the letter on the desk addressed to him.

Dear Adam,

If you find this letter, know that I am safe.

The candle factory caught on fire yesterday. The firefighters tried to put it out, but it was too late. Dad and hundreds of other people died.

My aunt and uncle are here. I'm headed north to stay with them. They're waiting outside now, so this is the last chance I'll have to talk to you. Maybe.

Keep the music box. I know you like it. But be careful. Its music predicts death. I'm sure of that now, though you probably know all about it already. The first time it played for me, my dog got hit crossing the street. The second time it played, my grandma died of a heart attack. And the last time it played was when you heard it through my window the other day, right before my dad and so many other people were killed.

My grandpa wanted me to have this music box. I loved him a lot, but I don't want it anymore. I

also don't want it to go to someone I don't trust, so I'm giving it to you.

I don't know if you'll find this letter, but I just have a feeling there's a chance. I don't know how to explain it, but I do.

I hope I'm right. And I hope we cross paths again.

> *Your friend,*
> *Jack*

Your friend. Adam reread the letter five times. He'd never felt so puzzled in his life.

He glanced at the other items on the desk. The candle resting in the candlestick looked and felt just like the ones Francine had given him. It smelled the same too, like lavender. Adam touched the wick of the candle. It was cold.

None of it made sense.

His gaze fell on the music box. He had been itching to inspect the item ever since he'd first heard its eerie music several weeks ago. Its handsome wood and carved features beckoned him closer. When he touched it, a tingle shot up his arm.

There was no way to wind it. Adam examined the top, the bottom, and all four sides thoroughly, but the box remained closed and silent.

Then he found initials carved smoothly into the bottom of one side, next to a tiny engraving of a compass rose: JCW.

CHAPTER SEVENTEEN

PERMUTATIONS

"Time traveling, huh?" repeated Victor.

The old man and Adam were sitting outside the shelter, Victor bundled snugly in his wheelchair and Adam on the curb. It was the first day of December, a sunny but chilly afternoon. Adam had to bury his hands inside his pockets for warmth. Even the sidewalk felt like ice. He shifted his legs every so often so his bottom wouldn't freeze. Beside him, Victor peeled an orange as he listened to Adam recount his time in the town of Candlewick.

Ever since Uncle Henry shot down Adam's stories as if they were make-believe, Adam was extra careful not to mention the snow globe to his uncle again, and especially not his strange travels through time. But the mysterious journeys kept him from sleeping at night. After his teacher sent home a note because he had fallen asleep twice in class, Adam was determined to solve the snow globe's mysteries once and for all, for his own sanity if nothing else. Even if that meant confiding in another adult.

He chose Victor because the trusted old man had told many whimsical stories of his own. Plus, as a former mathematician, he was the likeliest person to consider the possibility of time travel without swatting the idea down as if it were a whining mosquito.

Indeed, when Adam first brought up the notion, Victor merely answered, "There are many unexplored questions in this world. Who is to say time traveling is out of bounds?"

After Adam finished recounting his adventures with the magic snow globe, Victor nodded as if Adam had told him a completely ordinary story.

"What I am most perplexed about," said Victor, "is the music box. An object that predicts death could be very valuable—though I personally wouldn't like to own such a thing. Some knowledge is best left unknown."

Adam wasn't sure if he agreed. Such an item *would* be valuable, though from what he'd observed, the music box only appeared to play a warning tune—nothing more, nothing less. It didn't give any clues as to who, what, when, where, or how. More details would be helpful. If he could have foreseen exactly how and when his parents were going to die, for instance, he might have been able to save them. They'd still be living together now, in their spacious townhouse with a garden in the yard, sitting in front of the cheerful fireplace in the living room. His mother would volunteer at the school book fairs and show up at class parties like the other parents. His father would come in for Bring Your Parent to School Day. Adam would never again have to awkwardly explain to a new teacher that Uncle Henry was not his dad, but his uncle.

Victor shook his head and gave Adam a tiny smile. "Anything that has happened in the past has happened," he said, as if reading the boy's mind. "Thus, any changes you try to make now will have happened already, and bring you right back to where you are. The outcome, the present that we experience today, remains the same. That much I am sure of."

"How do you know?" insisted Adam.

"Well, it's sort of like permutations. Say you have three spoons—a bronze spoon, silver spoon, and gold spoon. You put the bronze and silver spoons down, in that order. Where does that leave the gold spoon?"

"Last—after the bronze one and the silver one."

"Right. The gold spoon can't go anywhere *but* last because of the other two spoons. That's one combination, and it represents our reality. Now, if you rearrange the order this time, and have the gold spoon be first or second, then you have a completely new combination. But then that combination represents a whole *other* reality, one we do not and cannot live in. Your name might not be Adam Lee Tripp in that world, wherever it is. I might not even be born."

"But . . ." Adam frowned. "Are you saying the past can't be changed?"

Victor held up an orange peel. "See this peel? Let's

say I accidentally drop it on the ground. It gets blown away in the wind and lands on someone's windshield. This startles the driver, and he swerves off the road. His car is now wrecked, so he misses his daughter's ballet recital because he has to wait for a tow truck."

Adam didn't see where this was going. "And then what?"

"Well, then the daughter, upon realizing that her dad isn't in the audience, performs terribly. Her teacher later evaluates the recital and ends up giving the lead in the next big performance to another dancer." Victor sucked in his breath. "So the daughter decides to travel back in time to prevent the orange peel from hitting the windshield. But then it turns out her appearing out of thin air was what startled me and made me *drop the orange peel in the first place!*"

"That's ridiculous," Adam argued.

"That is the paradox of time traveling. Everything up to today—to this very minute—has happened because of a specific series of events. *Including* anything that you try to change by going back. And I'm not saying the daughter did the wrong thing by traveling back in time," Victor added with a shrug. "It could be that during the big performance, a piece of scaffolding falls onstage and hits the lead dancer right in the foot. So she managed to save herself by avoiding a bigger disaster."

Adam wasn't completely following Victor's line of thinking. He wondered what seemingly small incident had caused Victor's university to lose funding and consequently make the former mathematician lose his career. Or what orange peel had caused his parents' plane to crash. Life certainly didn't seem fair.

"The thing I don't get," said Adam, changing the subject, "is who was J.C. Walsh? He's way older than both me and Jack. Jack would be in his forties right now, and J.C. Walsh looked to be at least sixty-something."

"Are you sure the initials *JCW* refer to the man you saw in October?"

"No . . . but who else could it be?" Adam explained again how the stranger in the raincoat had carried a snow globe into the Biscuit Basket and introduced himself as J.C. Walsh. "I haven't seen him since then," he added. "He must've not liked the red velvet cake."

"Naw, your uncle's baking is some of the best I've ever tasted," Victor reassured him. "Has the bakery reopened?"

"Tomorrow."

The broken window had finally been fixed after a long week. Uncle Henry was currently preparing special snowflake cookies for the Biscuit Basket's reopening. That reminded Adam—he had promised to help taste test the cookies later that night.

"I have to go," he told Victor. "Thanks for listening."

"Anytime, sonny."

As Adam slowly walked home, he considered the initials on the music box again. His first thought had been they stood for Jack's name—Jack Something Walsh. But Jack had said the music box was a gift from his grandpa. J.C. Walsh must've been Jack's grandfather, then. Except, according to the name on the headstone, *his* name had been Elbert Walsh.

Adam hopped over a puddle on the sidewalk. Maybe he could still track down Jack. But even as the thought crossed his mind for the hundredth time, he knew it was near impossible. Finding someone in the city of New York was hard enough, and his only lead there was Charlie. That had been a dead end. Extending his search to unknown towns and cities outside New York without the proper resources . . . well, he was out of luck.

Back at the bakery, Uncle Henry had finished baking the first batch of snowflake cookies. The careful baker had even made each one different to truly capture the unique quality of snowflakes: some cookies had six prongs, others twelve; some had crisscross patterns; still others had strange patterns in tartan and zigzag. Each cookie was lightly dusted with fine blue and white sprinkles.

The sight of the beautifully assorted cookies cheered up even Adam. "These look amazing, Uncle Henry," he said.

"Thank you, my boy. Here's to a new beginning for the Biscuit Basket. Whoever tried to knock us down failed. Tomorrow we will be back stronger than ever— just in time for the holidays!"

Adam helped himself to three cookies. The crunchy sugar reminded him of real snow. He couldn't wait for a snowfall to hit New York City.

Later, Adam went upstairs to his bedroom. After making sure the door was closed, he pulled open the bottom drawer of his dresser and carefully took out a golden disk attached to a fine golden chain.

It was the pendulum he'd pocketed from the ruins of the candle factory.

Adam studied the object. He'd managed to identify what it was when he returned home from his last journey and looked at it under proper lighting. The disk was smooth, and the chain looked almost brand-new. He knew, however, it was nearly a century old. The last owner he'd seen wearing it had been the Gold Mold's father, in 1922.

He had no doubt the item was extremely valuable. Worth hundreds at least, perhaps thousands. They could sell it and make a small fortune. But he knew he could never bring himself to do so. He'd seen its power first-hand, and the idea of letting it slip into some random person's possession didn't feel right.

The alarm clock on Adam's nightstand went off. He looked up in surprise. The time on the clock was wrong once again—as if the hour hand kept rewinding itself. It was the third time it had happened in the last few days. And it wasn't just the alarm clock. Uncle Henry's baking timer only worked sporadically, ever since Adam came home from the burned factory.

He placed the pendulum back inside the bottom drawer.

CHAPTER EIGHTEEN

A VIEW OF THE FIRE FROM THE OTHER SIDE

It's often said that those who don't learn from the past are doomed to repeat it. One particular family seemed to have missed this pearl of wisdom.

Robert Baron III had been as unpopular as his father, who in turn had been just as unpopular as *his* father, the first Robert Baron and founder of Candlewick's Candles. Like his predecessors, the third Robert Baron liked to strut around town in a tight, polished suit and sneer at the unfortunate people who weren't born into a family of wealth (and without whom his wealth would have been impossible). He was shrewd like a weasel and as sneaky as a rat. *Unlike* his predecessors, he was as lazy as a sloth and had an insatiable appetite, so much so that at least one button on his suit popped off daily. He was also fond of the golden pendulum he always wore around his neck, as it was a constant reminder to others of his enormous wealth, and a constant reminder to himself of his enormous power.

Every employee of Candlewick's Candles had a complaint or two about the factory. The floors of the factory were constantly covered in molten candle wax. There were open candle flames all around the cramped workspace, and it was common for the workers to accidentally burn their sleeves. More serious accidents had happened, too.

Yet somehow, all of those incidents were hushed up, forgotten. Formal complaints written against the factory disappeared mysteriously before they left the post office. Townspeople who had tried to form unions would abruptly forget their purpose and disband overnight.

As such, on the day of the disaster, when the boiler blew and the first licks of flame expanded across the factory, none of the workers thought of the greedy owner. If anything, they seemed to awake from some sort of deep trance. By then, the fire was spreading rapidly. Volunteer firefighters tried to put it out, to no avail. Water does not mix well with wax, and their attempts only fanned the flames outward in small bursts.

Afterward, it was revealed that Robert Baron III had been in enormous debt. A lavish lifestyle had laid waste to his inheritance, and his time overseeing the candle factory had not been as profitable as one might've imagined. After the fire, his mansion lay abandoned, most of his valuables were sold off, and his family name faded like smoke.

Only one individual knew the depth of the secrets

behind the factory owner's tyrannical grip on the townspeople. He alone knew why the workers had been so easily satisfied with the dreadful working conditions and worked so long for a cruel boss. In fact, this individual had been next in line to take over the factory, and would have ruled it with the same ruthless tactics, had it not burned down, and had Candlewick not become an abandoned wasteland.

Thirty years after the fire, in the ruins of his father's once-great estate, Robert Baron IV fumbled through the books and papers that remained in the dark library. A clear inch of dust had settled on the leather-bound volumes and richly patterned carpet, and built up inside the gilded frames of forgotten paintings. Outside the filthy windows, the moon cast its dim light on the black and deserted streets of Candlewick.

His long fingers paused on an old newspaper article dated from 1921. The page was yellow, and some of the text was nearly faded.

ELBERT THE EXCELLENT
REAPPEARS TO SHUN
CANDLEWICK'S CANDLES
May 22, 1921

New York, N.Y.—More than a decade after his rise and fall as a stage magician with a talent for hypnosis, thirty-year-old Elbert Walsh, formerly known as Elbert the Excellent, appeared in public again to denounce Candlewick's Candles, the highly successful enterprise owned by Mr. Robert Tweed Baron I and his son, Robert Tweed Baron II. "The swine cheated me," Walsh stated in an angry speech, which he delivered Saturday in a crowded downtown fish market. "The rights to those candles that you all love belong to me. And once I master the secrets of the time touch, Baron will be sorry."

When prompted to explain what exactly he meant by "time touch," the ex-magician refused to comment further.

It is known that the ex-magician used to work for a clockmaker.

"The time touch," Robert Baron IV murmured softly to himself. It wasn't the first time he'd come across this term. His father and grandfather often mentioned it at family reunions whenever business topics came up. They'd recount dreamily, over sparkling wine and fat cigars, how the first Robert Baron had secured the candles' formula from a lunatic—"the schmuck had no idea he was sitting on a fortune, and bless our great Baron name to have the insight."

They did agree, however, that one impressive thing about the schmuck had been his golden pendulum, which the first Robert Baron had had the presence of mind to steal when he'd ransacked the lunatic's apartment all those years ago. He didn't realize just how valuable it was until a group of butlers spontaneously broke into song and tap dance when he'd dangled the pendulum in the air.

"Great for keeping the workers in their place," Robert Baron II had crowed, putting his arms around his son's and grandson's shoulders. "Works well on officials, too. I've gotten out of paying for every single accident at the factory. The nifty thing helps you avoid giving pay raises, too."

Robert Baron IV stiffened at the memory. He never did find that nifty thing, despite searching every inch of the charred factory twenty years ago.

When he was a boy, he'd asked his family if they believed Great-Grandfather Robert I's theft of the pendulum would result in backlash or danger from the magician. They merely scoffed. "What's he going to do?" his grandfather had said. "The kid was cuckoo back then. Still is now. You know what his grand plan is? Claims he is going to reverse time and take back the candles. Says he's going to 'touch time' or some nonsense. Ha! Imagine if more people were like that pea-brain. I tell you, we're doing the working class a favor by keeping the wealth safe from them. The world does not need *their* kind. Steward! More wine, please."

Robert Baron IV carefully tucked the article into the pocket of his black suit, where he'd collected several dozen pages of notes on his quest to understand the phrase. Unlike his predecessors, he was far more cautious, and more open to certain possibilities. In the last two decades, he'd endlessly ruminated on how to restore his family's fortune and fame. The precious pendulum was missing, but perhaps there was another way. Time travel certainly *seemed* absurd, but if it existed, he knew it could be the answer to recovering his family's lost fortune. He could rewind the years and prevent the fire from happening, the same way Elbert had apparently sought to touch time and reverse it.

He unfolded one of those other notes and reread the short poem he had come across while conducting his research.

One in which all is foretold,
One in which lie gifts of gold,
One in which past days unfold.

He had gleaned the rhyme off an odd trio of travelers a few years ago. He'd chanced upon them in a dank tavern north of New York City, not far from Candlewick. After a few merry mugs of ale, the eldest of the travelers revealed to him that they were on a quest. For several years now, they had been trying to find three valuables that only a handful of people throughout history have known about. The trio had apparently gone all over the world in search of these treasures.

"The three treasures are all connected," her companion clarified, scratching his bushy beard.

"That's right, legend says time broke into three pieces long ago, and each piece is hidden somewhere in the world," said the third traveler, a middle-aged woman with a large backpack. The dim lightbulb hanging above her head revealed a small tattoo of a compass rose on the back of her neck, underneath strands of coarse hair that had come loose from her ponytail. On closer inspection, Robert Baron IV realized all three travelers bore the same insignia—on the wrist of the elderly woman, on the forearm of the man with the beard.

"We've been searching for one particular piece for about twenty years," the traveler continued. "Old Claudia here has searched for over seventy."

The wrinkled woman next to her nodded. "I was one of the first in the group," she said. "I'm the only one of us who knew the original founder. He was a brilliant man. An odd one for sure, but brilliant. He committed himself to the quest practically his entire lifetime, then suddenly quit. Said he'd finally come to terms with his past."

"Elbert the Eccentric," the others chuckled.

"He had a loyal following even after he retired, people dedicated to finding the treasures in his stead," continued the traveler with the backpack. "We all pay our respects any time we're in the area. He's buried not far from here."

"Of course, our group's membership has changed throughout the years," Claudia said. "But new and old members alike, we are all united in the search. We each have our own theories on what powers the pieces hold. You've heard such stories, I'm sure. Stories of cursed objects that bring death. Stories of strange people who pop up at random times throughout history, who never seem to age. Of course, most of those stories don't have much meat to them, details-wise, so for us they've ended up being dead ends. . . ."

"Well, there was *one* good lead," interjected the man with the bushy beard, banging his sloshing mug of beer on the counter. "A piping hot lead."

The woman with the backpack groaned. "Not this again, Sam——"

"Those humanitarians," the tipsy traveler went on. "You know they found something big, Marlene. Suddenly stopped joining us in our expeditions. Said they were taking a break. I knew something was fishy at the time. Should've made them explain themselves that night at their house——"

"You'll have to forgive us, Sam gets riled up easily," said the traveler called Marlene with an apologetic glance at the newcomer. "First of all, we have no proof. It was likely just a harmless toy——"

"It was real and you know it," argued Sam. "They found it on their own and kept quiet about it." He turned to Robert Baron IV and said, "When the Tripps wouldn't tell us anything, we questioned their neighbors. One of them had a story that the Tripps appeared from thin air one evening, wearing winter coats when it was eighty-five degrees out. And then another time, another person claimed to have met the Tripps—exactly as they were—*fifty* years ago as a child. Said they looked *exactly* the same."

Robert Baron IV had straightened up in his seat. "You're saying this—this object that your former comrades found—it allowed them to travel to the past?"

The three travelers glanced at one another uneasily. The tipsy traveler blurted, "Oh, to the devil with it!" With a hiccup, he turned in his stool, nearly falling off in the process, and said, "One of the pieces we were looking for is supposed to rewind time. And based on the stories, it sounds exactly like what Lin and Thomas Tripp had found."

"The rumors were indeed odd," murmured Claudia. "But even if they were true, I'm sure they had their reasons for not being forthcoming with us. They always liked helping people, and perhaps there was something that had more pressing needs than our simple fascination. Perhaps they realized the item was dangerous. Perhaps something that powerful can wreak havoc on the world." The old woman bowed her head. Her fingers tightened around the mug she held. "Either way, they died in a plane crash a few years ago, leaving behind a son. That little boy lost everything. We shouldn't speak ill of our lost comrades."

There was a somber silence.

"If the Tripps did have a piece of the time touch, I'm

sure they kept it on them at all times, and it likely broke in the rubble of the plane accident," sniffed Marlene. She clanked her empty mug on the counter. "So for all we know, the piece of time is out there, floating free again. And we know there are other pieces of the time touch out there, too. We'll keep looking. We won't give up." Then she looked at her backpack and sighed. "Although, I won't lie, sometimes I feel like giving up."

"What's meant to be will be," replied Claudia, folding her ancient hands together. "I've always said if you aren't meant to own something, it won't come to you. Same with the time touch. Something that magical must have a mind of its own, almost." She smiled at her friends. "Besides, what adventures we've had on the hunt, eh?"

The others murmured in agreement. At that point, the newcomer spoke up and quietly asked what the object the Tripps had been seen carrying looked like.

"It was a glass ball," answered the tipsy traveler. "A snow globe, wasn't it?"

To the dubious credit of the notorious Barons, each son had possessed a sharp memory, which was necessary for keeping track of all their blackmailing and legal loopholes. The last Baron, Robert Baron IV, used this ability to his advantage as he tracked down the elusive snow globe.

By the time he'd run into the trio of travelers, he'd

been painstakingly following clues for almost thirty years. He'd trailed people, asked questions, pursued leads, snuffed out dead ends. In an old antique shop, he'd devoured the tale of an oddly dressed boy with "glowing shoes" that was chronicled in a butcher's diary from the 1930s. In a recently published journal of unexplained phenomena, he'd come across a quote from an elderly fellow claiming to have witnessed a lad vanish in front of a Midtown pretzel cart sometime in the 1960s. Robert Baron IV latched on to these leads like a tick on to thick hair. He adopted a new moniker as he followed the trail: M for Mysterious—partly to conceal his identity, partly because it suited the nature of his secretive research, and partly because he lacked the imagination to come up with anything better.

When he'd found the Biscuit Basket, he almost laughed out loud. How ironic that the world's most valuable possession lay inside *that* shack of a place.

His first attempt at obtaining the item hadn't worked. He'd meant to bribe the wretched child for the snow globe, but the kid was stubborn. Horrible creatures, children were—he never understood why people wanted them. Maybe that was why his own father had never given him the time of day.

His second attempt hadn't worked either. Theft was harder than people made it out to be, especially when one must navigate a rickety bakery surrounded by dozens of customers.

So he had one option left. He would do what any self-respecting Baron would do, and what every self-respecting Baron had done to get what he wanted: he would put everything on the line. He needed that snow globe, no matter the cost.

The baker was still on high alert, he knew. He needed to lie low and wait. Then, when the right time came, he would strike like a serpent.

CHAPTER NINETEEN

THE FUTURE FRANCINE

On Friday evening after dinner, Adam checked the snow globe again for what seemed like the millionth time (but was actually the fifty-eighth) since his last visit to Candlewick.

Adam was prepared this time. He had gone to the library and scanned copies of the newspaper articles about the burned-down factory. He'd arranged the printouts neatly in a folder on his desk.

He'd also printed an article he found of his parents' plane accident.

That evening, when he opened his dresser drawer and peered hopefully inside, he was finally rewarded. Earlier that day, the snow globe had been blank. Now, a snowy cityscape of New York stood inside the glass. Adam's heart plummeted.

It's peculiar how sometimes the one thing we want badly makes us second-guess it once it's finally within our reach. Adam stared at the tiny skyscrapers. Fear rose in his stomach.

It's time, he decided. *For whatever's next.*

Adam grabbed his files and put them in his backpack. He glanced at the music box on his bed and grabbed the device too, just in case he was to meet Jack again. He took a deep breath, then shook the snow globe.

The next moment, he found himself in the middle of Central Park. The ground was covered with a sheet of snow; the bare tree branches along the trails crackled with brittle ice. Above him, the sky was an endless white.

Adam looked around. He didn't recognize anybody, nor did he know where to go. He read a sign nearby that said he was near Belvedere Castle, the miniature stone fortress that overlooked the surrounding treetops. As a biting wind picked up, Adam instinctively clutched the snow globe tighter and headed down the path toward the castle.

Belvedere Castle had been his father and Uncle Henry's favorite spot as children. Uncle Henry once recounted how the two brothers used to race up its stone steps and reenact plays, wars, and other games, bound only by the limits of their imaginations. They'd pretend to be kings of a fairy-tale land, and make believe the sun was a pot of gold, the clouds silver, and the park their kingdom.

"Those were the special days," Uncle Henry had told Adam. "Your father and I, we didn't have a care in the world. We would be late coming home for dinner because we'd lose track of time. Always felt as if time stopped for us when we played."

Adam had visited the castle with his uncle several years ago, but he had refused to go up because heights scared him, despite his uncle's promises that it was completely safe. Uncle Henry had given up visiting the castle after that.

The castle came into view. The three-story structure, with its impressive turret and walls, belonged more to a fairy tale than a modern-day park. For a moment, Adam felt his younger self whimper, felt a familiar tug at his chest. But he cast aside the fear. Slowly, using the snow globe for strength, he went up the narrow steps.

He emerged at the topmost level. The park and surrounding cityscape sprawled before him under a quiet blanket of snow. If it weren't for the branches in the distance, it was near impossible to tell where the sky ended and the ground began. He stood near the edge, breathlessly taking in the view that normally only birds could see, the distant trees no bigger than his thumb.

For the first time, Adam understood why his father and Uncle Henry liked this place so much.

There were a few other people enjoying the sights that day on top of the castle, some with cameras pointed at the scenery, some simply taking in the view.

"Well, heya, it's you," said a voice behind him. "The time traveler."

He turned and saw a dark-skinned woman standing

beside one of the stone railings, bundled in a flared gray coat and carrying a matching briefcase. Crinkles appeared in the corners of her eyes as she smiled at Adam. He knew that smile.

"Francine?" he said in disbelief.

"I was just taking a little lunchtime walk before going back to work," said Francine.

Adam had a mountain of questions, but what came out was, "To sell candles?"

Francine chuckled. "I don't do that anymore. Haven't for a long, long time. I work in an office now."

"Francine, what—what year is it?"

Francine answered. They were in December of 1960.

"I guess you came to comfort me," she continued. "That snow globe is truly magical, isn't it? It knows."

Adam was afraid to ask, but he swallowed hard and asked, "Is . . . is Tito okay?"

"Oh, it's not about Tito. He passed more than twenty years ago." Francine smiled sadly. "Shortly after the last time you visited."

Adam felt a wave of sadness clench his chest. "I'm sorry." He made a mental note to somehow obtain a polio vaccine for Tito the next time he traveled back far enough. That would be his goal after he safeguarded Candlewick. And after he rescued his parents.

"It's not your fault, Adam." Francine's expression was kind. "You're not the only one who's tried to save him. But magic can't solve all the world's ills."

"Huh?"

Francine motioned to a nearby bench, and the friends sat. "Believe it or not, you weren't the only time traveler to visit me in my childhood," she said. "In fact, I was visited by two others, several years before you came along. They were very kind. They wanted to cure Tito, among other things."

"Who were they?"

"I don't really know. They never told me much about themselves." Francine closed her eyes. "But they were a married couple. And they were from the future, just like you."

Adam desperately wanted to learn more, but his original goal weighed heavily on his mind. He didn't want to waste any time. The scene in the snow globe could vanish any second.

"Francine, before anything else, there's something I have to tell you. I need to warn the people of Candlewick about their future." Adam placed the snow globe on the ground, then rummaged inside his backpack for the file. "You need to give this to the police," he said, handing the file to Francine. "The Candlewick candle factory will burn down in seven years. A bunch of townspeople will die. And in 1992, my parents—my parents' plane—"

Francine examined the articles. "Nobody will believe this."

"They will," insisted Adam. "Please, Francine."

"It's not that simple. The past can't be changed. My sharing these with the police won't make a difference."

"What do you mean, the past can't be changed?" Adam was reminded of what Victor had said. "How do you know?"

"I've seen it with my own eyes, Adam. The other time travelers thought it could be, too. They tried to bring back a polio vaccine for Tito but could never get the timing right. There was no cure yet from their time period, you see, only a preventative vaccine, and Tito was already sick each time they visited. They tried to help him, and they tried to help me, too . . . but they couldn't."

"Help you how?"

Francine took a deep breath. "The first time the travelers met me, I was very young. It was before my parents passed. I was living in New Jersey at the time. The time travelers warned me that my parents would die at the carnival. They said they had been there—witnessed the whole thing. They wanted to prevent the tragedy."

For a moment, the only sound was the wind whistling in their ears.

"I was scared," said Francine, her voice quieter. "When the carnival came to town, I begged my parents not to go. And, seeing how upset I was, they didn't. But on the last day, the carnival invited everyone in for free. We didn't have a lot of money, you know, so we went. My parents and I went on the carousel. Slow and easy. But it turned out that was the ride that mal-functioned. I survived. Many others did not." Francine looked at her hands. "I remember the accident as if it were yesterday. I was seven at the time."

In the back of Adam's mind, he saw Francine as a child again. He could imagine her after the accident, numb and confused, same as he had been when he'd heard the news of his parents' plane crash. She'd likely have been in denial the first few nights, thinking her parents would return home any second with big smiles and saying, "Tricked you! We're all right!" Fast-forward a few years, Adam saw her selling candles in the cold streets, holding fast to the only family she knew—other lonely children who had suffered similar tragedies.

"At first, I blamed those adults for telling me," said Francine. "Most of all, I blamed myself. If I hadn't warned my parents, they might've gone to the carni-val a different day, and everything would've been fine." She looked pointedly at Adam. "But then again, maybe it wouldn't have been. Because when you think about it, the travelers warned me of what was to come—but what was to come had been recorded in history. So there wasn't any changing it. Not really."

A lump grew in Adam's throat. "Either way, it wasn't your fault."

Francine nodded. "It wasn't anyone's fault. I didn't understand it for a while, why things happen the way they do. I still don't. But I'm okay now. I have a loving

190

family and a good job. I've been okay for a long time. And one day, you will be too."

Anger coursed through Adam's insides. "No, the past has to be changed," he said in frustration. "It *has* to! We can stop accidents. We can even prevent wars, maybe. We can get our parents back!"

"Even if you can alter the past, something else would happen in its place," said Francine. "What if you'll want to change that too? You'll end up chasing the past until the day you die, without ever treasuring the golden moments of the present."

Adam didn't know what would happen if he managed to prevent the plane crash. Would the months and years after the crash disappear? Would time reset, and take him back to when he was five—back to their house in the suburbs, his parents alive this time?

But then the last seven years wouldn't have existed.

Adam thought of his uncle. He thought of the time he and Uncle Henry tried to make the world's tallest stack of pancakes in their apartment, and how it toppled just before it reached the ceiling. They had spent the rest of the morning laughing and eating and cleaning up the mess. He thought of every Christmas, when they'd stroll around Manhattan and listen to the holiday music piping from storefronts, until they both grew tired of hearing the tunes. Then they'd go home and Uncle Henry would make a batch of his special homemade cupcakes topped with candy cane sprinkles.

He thought of the simple days in the winter, when snow fell on everything and the entire city had a hushed feel. He'd stay indoors by the warm heater, playing chess or cards with Uncle Henry, or simply lolling on the floor with a blanket and a good book. He thought of Victor and listening to his brilliant stories out in the sunshine. He thought of the random strangers he'd met on the street, and the time someone dropped a wallet, which he returned.

Adam didn't say anything. Francine reached into her coat and revealed a handful of Bittersweet Bonbons. She handed the bunch to Adam. He brightened momentarily when he saw the delicious candies, but his mood was still cloudy. He kicked a pile of snow at his feet.

"You'll get your head around this one day," said Francine. "You're a smart kid." She nodded at the snow globe. "Time to go home."

Adam glanced at the empty snow globe on the ground. "Not yet," he said. "You said I'm here to comfort you about something."

"And you have. I have a good life, Adam, but every now and then we all feel a little lonely. You've reminded me I'm not alone. And you aren't alone, either." Francine stood and put Adam's file in her briefcase. "I'll see what I can do. Just for you. I'll give the town's fire department a phone call. But you shouldn't dwell on the past, Adam. You are who you are today because of it."

Her gaze fell on the snow globe. "Imagine, such an

innocent thing can hold so much power." She chuckled. "I have a feeling many people would love to get their hands on it—some for far more devious reasons than yours. They'd be disappointed to learn it won't do much for them."

She gently took the snow globe to examine it. Adam lunged forward, but it was too late. He watched in horror as the bright snow confetti swirled inside the glass.

Instead of vanishing, however, Francine simply stood there. Nothing happened. They both watched the sparkling confetti snowstorm inside the glass.

"It only works for specific people, I guess," Francine said, looking relieved.

A thought occurred to Adam. "The other time travelers, the ones you met in your childhood. They gave you the cassette player."

"That's right. They felt terrible about what happened to my parents. They felt terrible they couldn't do more, for me and for my friends. They gave us the player on one of their last trips, and as many batteries as they could carry. The other children and I played those tapes till they frayed."

Then another thought struck Adam, this time, like a firework. "The couple. Did they . . . did they look like . . . ?" He was suddenly at a loss for words.

Francine looked at him curiously. Then she leaned forward, peering at the boy as a great smile crossed her face.

"Yes, I believe so. Yes, that makes perfect sense." Francine reached out and grabbed Adam's hand. "Thanks for being a good friend, Adam. Your parents would be proud of you."

Francine placed the swirling snow globe back in Adam's hands. Before he could reply, Francine and Central Park disappeared.

Adam was back in his bedroom, the snow globe and Bittersweet Bonbons in his hands.

CHAPTER TWENTY

DISTINCTIVELY DECEMBER

Winter is the one time of year when everything slows down, willingly or otherwise. Animals are naturally aware of the season's lethargic effects and promptly respond by hibernating in a cozy area until warmer weather comes. Humans, strangely enough, tend to ignore the slump altogether by working the same as they always have, if not more. In the northern hemisphere especially, it is strange how deadlines tend to be set for the end of the year, right in the freezing heart of winter, when all you want to do is curl up with a nice, hot cup of cocoa and a warm blanket.

In the second week of December, Adam's school flooded its students with end-of-semester tests. Spelling tests, geography tests, reading tests, test tests, and so on and so forth. Outside of school, Adam was kept busy handling the stream of customers at the bustling bakery. The break-in a few weeks ago was quickly forgotten. With the arrival of the winter holidays, Uncle Henry whipped up piles of deep-fried doughnuts and flaky rugelach for Hanukkah, and took in mounting orders of gingerbread men, snowflake cookies, and fruitcake for Christmas.

Why anyone liked fruitcake was beyond Adam. But we digress.

The magic snow globe, the music box, and the pendulum lay quietly inside Adam's dresser for a week. So it came as a great shock on Sunday evening, long after Adam had fallen asleep, when the music box suddenly went off.

He sat up in bed. The muffled, eerie melody, which had previously captivated him and inspired a sense of wonder, now filled him with dread. He jumped up to open the drawer. The music magnified in the open air.

Uncle Henry's snores broke off in the living room.

"What's that sound?" Adam heard his uncle mumble sleepily.

Adam tried to close the music box. The lid wouldn't shut.

The melody continued to play, conjuring bleak images that made Adam more panicked with each passing second. He pushed on the lid with all his strength, but it was stuck. He tried turning the box over and pushing from the bottom, but it was no use.

That was when Adam saw that the initials on the bottom of the box no longer read *JCW*, but *ALT*.

Adam Lee Tripp.

Uncle Henry entered the room just as the melody finally faded.

"Adam? Everything all right in here? It's two in the morning."

Adam trembled. He couldn't speak.

"Adam?"

"Uncle Henry . . ." Adam swallowed and looked down at the music box in his hands. "Something bad is going to happen."

"What? Oh. I see." Uncle Henry gave an understanding nod. "You had a nightmare. Don't worry, boy, bad dreams can't hurt you." He glanced at the music box, and had he not been in such a sleepy state, he might have wondered where his nephew had gotten it. "Music does help soothe the mind after a nightmare, but I'm not sure that particular melody helps."

"No, you don't understand! Someone is going to *die!*"

Adam tried to explain how the music box was bad luck. But he couldn't tell the full story unless he explained how he found Jack's letter through the traveling snow globe, and the last time he'd tried to explain the snow globe's powers to his uncle, it hadn't gone so well. Then again, he reasoned, this was a matter of life and death. So he told Uncle Henry the truth. Again.

His version sounded jumbled, even to himself, and seemed as if he'd made everything up. A nightmare certainly was the easier explanation. Worried, Uncle Henry coaxed him back to bed and said they'd talk about it in the morning. The next day, he secretly made a call to Adam's school counselor.

Now, as much as Ms. Ginger prided herself on finding an easy solution to every problem, her true joy came from whipping kids into shape, one way or another. You could take a pair of troublemakers to her, and she'd mold them right into little angels, with a few minor scars.

What kind of scars, you ask? About seven months ago, the then-infamous fifth grader Roger Daly had been sent to Ms. Ginger's office for disrupting class one too many times. Nobody knew what had happened behind the closed door, but Roger emerged from the room clutching his ears and moaning, "Too much talking, too much talking." From that day on, whenever he saw Ms. Ginger in the hallway, he'd duck, cover his ears, and run off in the other direction.

As stated before, Adam's shyness had always been of particular interest to the school counselor. He was not a troublemaker, but his teachers all agreed the boy was much too quiet. Ms. Ginger firmly believed only she could wheedle Adam out of his shell and transform him into a sociable boy, like her own darling sons.

On the day of Adam's appointment, she sat in her office with her back straight and her pencils sharpened. Her red suit matched her lipstick, and her flaming red hair was tied back in an orderly bun. Hung against the wall behind her desk were various plaques and awards, each of enormous pride for Ms. Ginger:

- *Perfect Attendance Award*
- *Ninth-Place Speed Reader in the Manhattan Women's Book Club for Impressive School Guidance Counselors Aged 30–35* [1]
- *Fourth-to-Last-Place Finisher of the Central Park Mile Race*
- *Runner-Up to the Employee of the Month Award, March 1990*
- What looked like a framed letter from an editor at a short stories magazine that read, *"Although we appreciate your unusual and slightly confusing tale about a guidance counselor with superpowers who turns bratty children into snakes, we unfortunately must decline your submission."* [2]

When Adam entered, Ms. Ginger gave him a bright red, falsely cheery smile. Adam did not return the smile. He had been to Ms. Ginger's office several times before, and each time, the school counselor had given him the same useless advice—"Join an after-school club!"—without thinking about Adam's limited time

---

[1] There were only eleven people in that particular book club
[2] Ms. Ginger liked to show people this particular letter as proof she had a knack for writing unique stories.

and resources. Not to mention the guidance counselor tended to ramble with doting stories about her two sons, one of whom was in the same class as Adam and had stolen Adam's favorite pen in the fourth grade.

"Your uncle tells me you've been having nightmares," said Ms. Ginger as she opened her spiral notebook to a blank page. "Why don't you tell me about them?"

Adam sucked in his breath, then exhaled. He might as well try. "I have this music box," he began. "It—"

"A music box?" interrupted Ms. Ginger. "Children older than five should not play with music boxes, in my opinion. Ridiculous toys with silly melodies. Weakens the mind. My sons stopped playing with toys when they were three years old." The guidance counselor tutted to herself and scribbled down some notes. "Go on."

"The music box," Adam began again, "is bad luck. I think whenever it plays. . . someone dies."

Ms. Ginger dismissed this. "Now, Adam, as a professionally licensed counselor, with two darling sons of my own, I know *exactly* how children think," she said. "Kids make up these superstitions and let their imagination carry them into the wild. That is why I personally don't allow my own children to read fiction books. Fills up their heads with nonsense. If it were up to me, I'd fire the idiotic school librarian and replace the fiction stacks with good old textbooks."

Adam had heard this same tirade before. Ms. Ginger

cleared her throat and patted her bun to make sure it was securely in place.

"Now, Adam," she said again. She leaned forward in her seat and clasped her hands together. "I am going to recommend you let go of anything silly that's floating about in your head. There is no room in this life for ridiculous whims."

Normally, Adam would nod and mumble, "Yes, ma'am." But over the past two months, something had changed in the twelve-year-old. He looked up at the stern grown-up and said firmly, surprising even himself, "There are many possibilities in life, Ms. Ginger."

Ms. Ginger was taken aback as well. "I beg your pardon?"

"We don't know the answer to everything," said Adam, growing more courageous. "There could be magic hidden in places we didn't think of before."

The guidance counselor scrunched her eyebrows and studied Adam as if trying to figure out whether the boy was making fun of her.

"Adam, magic is not real," Ms. Ginger said slowly, each syllable drawn out as if she were speaking to a toddler.

"You don't know that!" argued Adam. "It's real. I *know* it is. And I know someone's going to die!"

Two things happened later that day. The first was Ms. Ginger's happy reassurance that Adam was fine. "It was the first time I've seen Adam speak up," she reported to

Uncle Henry. "You're very welcome! I'd say it was the proudest moment of my career—aside from the time I met the governor's pet poodle; did you know I was featured in the newspaper with that pooch? My name was in there, right in the caption. Anyhoo, you're welcome again, and please do call with anything you need in the future!"

The second thing that happened was a bit darker. The music box predicted correctly—there was indeed a death that night.

After school, Adam ran straight for the shelter. He didn't stop running until he hurried inside the building and panted, "Victor!"

Victor and two women were chopping up cabbages in the kitchen for that night's dinner. When the old man saw Adam, he waved and gave his usual toothless grin.

"Hello, fellow!" he replied. "Good to see—"

"Victor, I have to talk to you in private," interrupted Adam. "It's urgent."

The two women exchanged curious glances. Victor nodded and scooted across the room in his wheelchair. "I'll be right back, ladies," he told them before escorting Adam down the hallway to his room in the back.

"What is it, sonny?" asked Victor after he shut the door.

"Remember the music box? The one I found in

Candlewick with Jack's letter? The one that predicts death."

"Ah yes, I remember."

"It played last night, Victor. Someone is going to die."

Victor wrinkled his nose. "Not necessarily," he began, but Adam shook his head.

"I'm *positive*," insisted Adam. "Jack told me." He recounted how the music box had played for Jack before his dog, grandmother, and father died. He mentioned how his own initials mysteriously replaced *JCW*'s on the bottom of the box. "It's magic. I don't know when, or how, but someone I know is going to die." His lip trembled.

Adam didn't say aloud who it might be, but he didn't need to. Victor understood.

"Your uncle is in good health, last I saw," the old man reassured him. "The chances of something happening to him are slim. The music box might simply be telling you that all humans are mortal, and that eventually, everyone's time comes."

Adam bit his lip.

"Go on home, sonny," Victor said, placing a hand on Adam's shoulder. "Make sure the door at home is locked if you're worried."

Adam nodded miserably, then left the room.

Victor sat by himself for several long moments. The old man gazed out the foggy window, deep in thought.

He had guessed correctly that the music box was

trouble. Over the last fifty years, he'd told his share of extraordinary tales, some scarier than others. Yet it was not ghosts, or dragons, or three-headed monsters with the ability to swallow people in one gulp that were the most frightening. Those paled in comparison to the one simple fear that had plagued humans since the dawn of time. He'd seen powerful adults crumble and handsome young men morph into deranged lunatics, tortured into insanity, as they tried in vain to avoid the one thing that all flowers, squirrels, and pigeons—and people—must face eventually.

The old man wheeled back down the hallway to the kitchen. When the others asked him what the twelve-year-old had wanted, he refused to say, and merely answered, "Only time will tell."

CHAPTER TWENTY-ONE

M IS FOR MURDER

Adam stayed awake past his bedtime. Two hours and three minutes past his bedtime, to be exact.

It was after midnight, the quiet time when all is still, and every action becomes suspicious tenfold. If your doorbell rings in the morning, that is as ordinary as puddles after a rainstorm, but if your doorbell rings in the dead of night, you'll think twice before answering. If you're digging a hole during the day, you might get a few good-natured people asking questions about what you're doing. But if you're digging a hole past midnight, you can be sure the police will arrive with questions (and possibly handcuffs), and they *won't* be good-natured.

Adam listened to Uncle Henry's steady snores coming from the living room. He turned on his side and pressed his ear against the pillow. He counted the number of cracks and peeling spots on the wall. His eyes felt like heavy lead weights, but he couldn't sleep.

Victor was right, he thought. *An object that warns of death is terrible.* The warning alone was enough to frighten him more than anything ever did, and made him want to crawl under his bed. Except he was too old for that. So he made do with huddling under his blanket.

"Maybe it's not going to be Uncle Henry," he mumbled to himself for the fortieth time. "Maybe it's Jack, or Daisy, or Francine, if she's still alive, or . . ."

His gut, however, told him it wouldn't be any of them. No, it would be someone closer to him.

The thought of Jack and Daisy tied his stomach into knuckle-sized knots. He couldn't prevent their families' deaths—even the notorious Robert Baron III didn't deserve to *die.* He never got the chance to intervene in his own parents' deaths. What was the point of owning something that could travel back in time, then, if it couldn't save lives?

His mind wandered to seven years ago, the day of the plane crash. He'd been sitting awake in his bedroom, waiting for his parents, when the grown-ups from social services arrived to deliver the news. They told him his parents wouldn't return, and that he would be moving to New York City to live with his uncle. They said other stuff too, but Adam didn't understand. Their words sounded far away, as if the grown-ups were speaking underwater. Within days, Adam had been thrown from his comfortable, familiar home into a chaotic world of long meetings with lawyers, of strange grown-ups asking him how he was twenty times a day, of new, cramped spaces.

He had started building himself a cocoon after that. It was where he could remain safe from all the changes. But, as Adam was now realizing, he couldn't avoid change any more than he could stay cocooned forever.

Francine and Victor had been right: there were memories he cherished, even after his parents' death.

A sudden loud crash downstairs made Adam sit upright. Uncle Henry was still snoring. His heart jumping in his chest, Adam opened his bedroom door a crack and strained his ears.

Muffled footsteps were coming up the creaky stairs from the bakery.

Fear rooted Adam to the spot. His heart now hammered in his chest—*pitter-patter-pitter-patter*—echoing in his eardrums and drowning out every other noise.

"*Uncle Henry!*" he tried to cry out, but the words stuck in his throat.

Someone fiddled with the doorknob on their apartment door. The puny knob lock clicked forward.

What happened next seemed to be in slow motion.

The door swung partly open, halted by the chain lock holding it in place.

Uncle Henry awoke mid-snore on the futon. "*Hrmph? What . . . ?*"

Long fingers pinching a pair of heavy-duty pliers

reached through the door crack. In a second, the chain lock had been cut clear in half. The door thundered open.

This all happened within the span of five seconds. By the time Uncle Henry stood up with a start, and by the time Adam could regain his senses, the intruder had leaped forward.

Adam watched his uncle fall to the floor with a thud. The intruder—tall, dark suit, sharp chin—pinned down his uncle with his foot and whacked the squirming baker's head with the pliers. Uncle Henry moved no more. Adam screamed.

The intruder turned to look at him. His hungry scowl sliced white in the dim light from the windows.

"Where is the snow globe?" barked M.

Adam slammed the door. On second thought, it probably wasn't the best course of action, because now he was trapped in his bedroom.

He leaped toward the single window, which faced the back alley. Their apartment was only on the second story, but the cement ground below seemed miles away. A jump down would very likely break his leg.

His bedroom door swung open. Adam threw whatever he could at M—his library books, his pencil case. Each futile projectile only bounced off M and made the man madder. He snatched Adam's arm and thrust him to the floor. Adam's nose hit the edge of his bedpost when he fell forward. It started to bleed.

"Enough! Where is the snow globe?" M jerked Adam backward.

Adam scrambled for something else to attack M with. With his free hand, he threw his pillow, which M tossed aside easily. The man shook Adam again.

"You of all people should know how it feels to lose everything," M hissed. "To lose your family and your home to a simple accident. We can turn it around. You can get your parents back. All you have to do is give me the snow globe."

Adam knew it would take one swing of M's pliers to knock him out like his uncle. He braced himself for the painful blow. A desperate idea formed in his mind—if he kept talking, maybe he could distract M.

"You can't prevent all accidents," he said, his voice shaking. "The snow globe is useless. People have already tried, believe me."

"Hmph, I don't expect a half-witted child like you to understand the snow globe's true potential. *You* only used it so you could vanish and dazzle your stupid friends, didn't you?"

"I don't have any friends," was Adam's response.

"Really now?" M's lips curled upward in a sneer. "That's not what I found in my investigations. My dim-witted aunt was quite fond of you. Her name's Daisy. You might remember her."

Adam froze. "Daisy?"

"She mentioned a boy, a 'wonderfully kind' boy,

who traveled from the future and encouraged her in her youth. If only she foresaw how useful the snow globe was, she could have taken it from you right then and there . . . For thirty-one years, I've tried to track down this item. You don't know all the hard work I've put into my quest, all those years of following endless leads. But now, I'm so close." M leaned forward, his eyes wild. "*So close,*" he repeated, "to bringing back everything I lost in the fire. To bringing back the destiny I was meant to have, what was taken from me so unfairly."

The fire. Daisy. Aunt. It took Adam only a second to connect the dots. "Candlewick's Candles," he gasped in spite of himself.

M nodded. "I was its next heir. But it's all gone. Nobody could find my father's body in the mess. Not that it mattered—the ungrateful townspeople didn't even show up for his memorial." M's face grew tense. His next words were barely a whisper. "With the snow globe in my possession, I can recover the fortune, grow it exponentially. I'll be the wealthiest man in the country. I'll even see my father again, and show him what *I* could accomplish. Candlewick's Candles will be an empire once again!"

"But you can't prevent his death," said Adam solemnly, thinking of Francine's words. "It's recorded history."

M's scowl returned. "Shut up, you imbecile. I'm asking you one last time—the snow globe, *where is it?*"

M began flipping aside the stuff on Adam's desk. Adam's gaze flicked involuntarily to the dresser. M's eyes narrowed, and he kicked the bottom drawer open. His grip on Adam loosened when he saw what was inside.

"*The pendulum!*"

M grasped the object with shaking fingers. The golden disk swayed on the chain.

"So *this* is where it went—proof of the snow globe's magic!"

Stall him, Adam thought pleadingly. *Help me stall him.*

For a moment, M seemed to be mesmerized. The villain stared at the pendulum. "Father?"

Adam wasn't sure whether he misheard. But M said it again.

"Father, it's me." M seemed to be talking to the pendulum. There was a breath of silence. "It's me, your son. The heir to the Baron name."

Then someone thrust M backward. M made a gagging noise and tried to push away the arm binding his throat. Adam broke free from M's grip and watched in shock.

"Victor?" he cried.

The elderly man was supporting his weight with a cane in one hand; his other arm was locked around M's throat. M swung the sharp pliers in his hand and jabbed the side of Victor's body. With a yelp, Victor let go and doubled over.

But the distraction allowed Adam to grab his music box from his drawer. He now smashed the wooden box on M, straight in his face. M howled in pain, dropping the pliers and the pendulum. Adam snatched the pliers and whacked M's head.

M was unconscious before he crumpled to the floor.

Victor was also on the floor, clutching his bad leg. The side of his sweatshirt was stained dark red.

Panicked, Adam rushed for the telephone and dialed 9-1-1, his nose still dripping blood. He found that his uncle was still knocked out cold, but breathing. Adam spoke with the operator, surprised they managed to understand him through his incoherent babbling. After shakily giving the operator the address and requesting an ambulance, he hung up and bent down next to Victor.

"Sorry I was late, sonny," Victor wheezed. "Couldn't get up the stairs in my wheelchair. Had to use my walking stick . . ."

"How'd you know we were being attacked?"

"I kept an eye out down the street. Saw a shady person breaking in, so I followed." Victor gave a shaky cough. "How's your uncle?"

"He's okay," Adam whispered. "The ambulance is coming. We'll get you and Uncle Henry to a hospital in no time. It'll be okay."

The red stain was growing larger. Adam grabbed a towel from the bathroom and pressed on the wound.

Victor gasped for breath and managed a toothless grin. "Listen, sonny, there's no need. I'm already old as it is . . . old and frail . . ."

"We can save you," Adam said, pressing the towel

harder. Tears pooled in his eyes. He blinked them away angrily. "Just hang tight, you'll be fine."

"The music box. . . . Remember what you told me? This was foretold."

"You won't die!" Adam shouted.

"My time would've come eventually one of these days, Adam . . ." Victor's voice was fading between the rasps. "I'm glad I got to save a life in the process."

"No, you're going to make it. Just hold on, the ambulance is coming . . ."

Victor clasped Adam's hand and said nothing more. After a few moments, his hand grew limp. All that was left was the faint trace of a smile on his wrinkled face.

CHAPTER TWENTY-TWO

OF WAITING ROOMS AND CEMETERIES

Adam had only been to the hospital once in his life. He had been eight years old at the time, and had accidentally burned his hand by spilling boiling water from the stove. He remembered hating the hospital's hallways, with their smell of disinfectant and their colorless floors, and the waiting room full of crying infants and uncomfortable plastic chairs. Most of all, he hated the harsh fluorescent lights and windowless walls.

He sat in a windowless waiting room now, watching a toddler tear apart the pages of a golf magazine. Adam didn't say anything (he probably would've torn out the pages too, as it was more fun than reading about golf) and merely sat there, silently counting down the hours on the clock. He had slept in the same waiting room the night before, and had somewhat gotten used to the smell and the bright lights. His neck was sore. The plastic chairs proved uncomfortable for sitting, and even more difficult for sleeping.

The events of the terrible night M attacked seemed like forever ago. In fact, only two days had passed on the calendar. Today was the day Uncle Henry would finally be released from the hospital. Adam didn't remember the exact words the doctor had used, but he'd heard the phrases "severe concussion" and "two-night mandatory stay."

A nurse appeared in the waiting room. "Adam?" she said with a smile. "Your uncle wants to see you."

Uncle Henry sat on a tiny bed with white sheets in a matching white room, eating a cup of chocolate pudding. His head was still bandaged, his face gaunt and his eyes heavy, but he brightened upon seeing Adam.

"They've been feeding me chocolate pudding nonstop," said Uncle Henry, waving his spoon. "Maybe I should extend my stay."

Adam and his uncle had talked a bit the previous day, but Uncle Henry had been less than coherent. Now the baker looked and sounded much healthier.

"Tell me the news about M again," said Uncle Henry.

"The police said he has a nasty bruise on his face and a broken nose. They've arrested him for breaking into our home, among other—stuff—" Adam's voice broke. He looked away.

"I should've taken you seriously when you told me about M." Uncle Henry touched his bandage and winced. "Experience is a tough teacher."

"I get why he did it, though," Adam said quietly. "He lost a lot. He wanted to change the past, like I did."

Despite all the terrible damage M had done, Adam understood the villain's motives, however misguided they'd been. In the end, they'd wanted similar things. But whereas Adam wanted to help others with the snow globe, M did not care if others were hurt in his quest.

Uncle Henry asked more about Adam's music box, which led to questions about the snow globe. This time, he fully believed Adam's tales.

"So M was trying to go back in time to stop the fire at the candle factory," Uncle Henry murmured.

Adam nodded, thinking of Victor's permutations. "I don't think it would've worked," he said. "What happens in the past can't be changed. It's like reading through a history textbook. Everything that's already happened up to this point has already happened. The only thing we can do is move forward."

"Yes, that makes sense."

"Also, the snow globe doesn't just take you where you want to go," Adam added. "It's really random."

Both random and logical, he thought. All the people he met were connected like the intricate arms of a snow-flake. He wondered where his parents had gotten the snow globe originally, and asked if his uncle knew.

"I recall hearing about it once," answered Uncle Henry. "They brought it back with them from a trip overseas. Were adamant they protect it with their lives. They hinted they wanted to use it to change the world for good. At the time, I'd just thought they meant it was worth a lot of money." He paused. "A time traveling snow globe. It doesn't surprise me that your parents owned such an item."

"The man in the raincoat who came into our bakery a few months ago—J.C. Walsh—he had one that looked identical to theirs," said Adam. "He was the one who told me to find it in the attic."

"He told you to find it?"

"Well, not exactly. He never told me what I was supposed to be looking *for*. Just told me to go to the attic, and that my adventures await."

"Hm, that's odd. Maybe he was friends with your parents." Uncle Henry looked thoughtful. "I guess we'll never know."

They both fell quiet. Uncle Henry took a few more bites of pudding.

Adam remembered something. "The Hol—the homeless shelter is holding a memorial service for Victor next week. On Christmas Eve."

"We'll be there," his uncle reassured him. "I'll be right as rain by then. Victor will be missed." Uncle Henry gingerly touched his bandages. "If he hadn't been there to save us, we would've both been goners. Not to say you didn't put up a good fight, from what I heard."

"The music box helped. Turns out it was great for throwing at people."

Adam studied the floor, thinking. The whole debacle had started with the music box, warning him of an

217

impending death, which he had told Victor about in a panic. Which had sent Victor looking after them, which had led to his death.

Victor's story about the orange peel came to Adam's mind. *All because of the piece of orange peel.* What was the orange peel in this case? The music box? Candlewick? The snow globe?

In the end, Adam kept these questions to himself. Uncle Henry looked like he needed time to recover from all the stories, on top of his injuries.

The rest of the week passed. Adam had no classes, due to winter break. He helped his uncle with the Biscuit Basket's reopening Friday. By then, news of the most recent break-in had spread, and the regulars that the bakery had amassed were waiting in droves. All day long, the place was full of friendly faces, welcome-back flower bouquets, and the pleasant smell of warm pastries.

When Adam went to bed that night, his stomach full of gingerbread, he thought of something else he hadn't told Uncle Henry.

The day after M attacked, while Uncle Henry was recovering in the hospital, Adam had briefly gone back to their apartment to snatch his pajamas and a book for the overnight stay in the waiting room. The music box lay against the foot of his bed, not a scratch on the wood.

The glistening pendulum lay next to it. It was then that he decided to check on the magical snow globe inside his drawer.

The inside of the snow globe had changed again, back to Candlewick Cemetery.

Adam had pondered for a solid ten minutes before he made his decision. Earlier, he wanted nothing to do with the snow globe or the music box ever again. But then he zipped up his jacket, picked up the snow globe, and gave it a good shake.

He found himself once more at the entrance to the cemetery. This time, the weather was clear. He saw a little girl in the distance, standing beside one of the gravestones. She wore a familiar white dress.

At first Adam felt nervous approaching this strange girl who hung out alone in a sea of headstones. But then he quickly realized it was none other than Daisy.

He was back in the 1920s. Above him, the sky was soft pink and blue.

"Hey, Daisy!" he called.

Daisy looked up at him with startled, round eyes. "How do you know my name?"

"What do you mean? We've met before. I'm Adam, remember?"

Daisy continued to look at him in amazement. Adam understood.

Daisy hadn't met him yet.

"Nobody comes here this early in the morning," said

the little girl. She motioned to the cemetery around her. "Are you here to visit someone?"

"Oh, no, my parents aren't buried here." Adam's voice faltered, but under Daisy's curious gaze, he went on, "They're at a different cemetery."

"How did your parents die?" she asked.

"They . . . died in a plane crash."

The truth would always be sad. But saying the words aloud to Daisy, it was as if an invisible weight that had been crushing Adam's chest had lifted. He would always remember that fateful day, but it was only one brief moment on the timeline, a timeline that held a million other moments, connecting a million other people. A timeline that continued to unfold with infinite possibilities. He would no longer dwell on a single point in the past. He was going to be truly open to the future. His parents would have wanted that.

He glanced at the name on the gravestone in front of Daisy, and said, "Your grandma, right?"

Daisy nodded.

Adam clasped Daisy's hand. For a few moments, neither of them spoke.

"She was my best friend," Daisy said softly. "We made all kinds of meals together. I don't have any other friends. Besides my cat, Dr. Tabbypaws."

"You'll meet new people one day," Adam promised. "There's a whole world out there. You like cooking, don't you?"

Daisy nodded again.

"One day you'll make a friend in New York City. She's a bit younger than you, but age doesn't matter when it comes to friendship. She says you make the best candies ever. I agree. I've tried them myself."

Daisy looked at him with wide eyes. "How do you know this?"

"The snow globe showed me." Adam held up the snow globe with the tiny cemetery inside. "It belonged to my parents. It connects me to people, you see, from different times and different places."

"Like magic?"

"Yes." Adam went on to describe some of the adventures he'd had. Daisy listened in awe, and laughed when he described Charlie and his menacing eye patch.

"When it's empty, it means it's time for me to go," Adam finished.

Daisy suddenly looked worried. "You're going to leave?"

"I'll be back."

"When?"

Adam gave her a mysterious smile. "How about this? On the fourth Monday of May, at eleven o'clock in the morning, come outside and look for me in the garden by your house."

"Really?" whispered Daisy. A smile lit up her face. "Does this mean we're friends?"

Friends. There was that word again, one that had once seemed so foreign to Adam. But his cocoon days were over.

"Yes," he answered. "We are friends. I might not see you every day, but remember: you're not alone." He held up the snow globe. *"We're not alone."*

"We are not," agreed Daisy. Adam was reminded again how smart the five-year-old was.

The snow globe had turned empty again, and he knew his work there was done.

Before he shook the snow globe, he said, "One more thing. If someone is upset, what do you think is the best way to cheer them up?"

The little girl thought for a few moments. "I think a little bit of candy never hurts," she said wisely, a spark of inspiration in her eyes. "Some sweet to temper the bitter."

Adam thought that was the last he'd see of Daisy. He was wrong, of course. Though he didn't know it at the time, in ten years he'd see her once more. But not through the snow globe. Rather, he'd find her in a town not far from Candlewick, thanks to a quick search on the rapidly developing apparatus called the Internet. Daisy would be recently retired from running a successful candy shop in Manhattan. She would welcome him warmly, and introduce him to her brilliant granddaughter, Rose, who was Adam's age and made sweets just as well as Daisy did.

And the three of them would sit and laugh and munch on bonbons into the night.

CHAPTER TWENTY-THREE

CLOSING THE TIME LOOP

Christmas Eve was a sight to see at the homeless shelter down the street. Adam had spent the morning helping decorate the place with vibrant lights and evergreen garlands. By the time of Victor's memorial service, the building looked not so much like a run-down residence but more like a gingerbread house, with striped candy canes hanging from the wood panels, and colorful droplets of light woven through the white snow on the rooftop. A perfect green wreath balanced on the front door.

"The Hole isn't really much of a hole anymore, is it?" said Uncle Henry as they admired the view.

"Don't call it that, Uncle Henry."

"You're right. It's not very respectful."

"No." Adam toed the pile of snow lining the edge of the sidewalk. "It's not a hole. It's a place for people to go when they're lost, like"—he raised his head—"a lighthouse. A candle."

"A candle," murmured Uncle Henry with a nod.

The service went well. Adam even went up in front of the room and said a few words, something he wouldn't have dreamed of doing a few months ago. The audience was a bit bemused by his speech on orange peels and permutations. But Adam knew every word he'd said was from the heart.

And that was when Adam fully understood that the snow globe was never meant to change the past.

From Francine, to Jack, to Daisy, to Robert Baron IV, the snow globe had instead shown Adam the ways in which people from every year and generation shared the same thoughts and fears. How they lost loved ones and had pasts they wished to change. But in the end, the clock only ticked onward, and that was the direction they needed to go. Including himself.

Later, in his room, he opened his drawer. The snow globe, the music box, and the pendulum rested peacefully in the white moonlight. The three pieces of time—past, future, and present. Jack's grandpa had been right about the legend. Adam, who knew of the enormous power inside each object, couldn't believe how harmless they looked now. Perhaps power was only dangerous when it was wielded incorrectly.

He took them aside one by one.

Adam made one more trip to the attic that year, on that very evening, to store the snow globe and the music box safely away. He had no need for either anymore. The snow globe he'd keep hidden until he and J.C. Walsh met again. He had a good feeling they would. And he'd keep the music box hidden until then as well. Like Victor had said, some knowledge was best left unknown. And perhaps J.C. Walsh had a good-hearted grandchild to whom he could entrust this family heirloom.

That left the pendulum. Even now, the gold seemed to enchant Adam. He had to make sure it never fell into the wrong hands. He needed to conceal it someplace where no one would think to look for its glitter. Adam thought again of Jack's grandfather and his magical ideas of time. A smile grew on his face. He knew exactly where to hide the pendulum: a place so obvious that even those searching for it wouldn't think to look there.

He found Uncle Henry reading in the living room, and the two made plans to visit Candlewick Cemetery as soon as spring arrived.

At bedtime, he bid his uncle good night, then went to sleep. It was the night before Christmas.

Elbert Walsh looked outside his window. It was snowing.

Behind him, two white-and-green-striped candles lit the dim room, casting long shadows on the piles of maps and journals across the table. Those had been from his early days, days spent traveling the world in search of the elusive piece of the time touch that could right the wrongs he'd endured.

Fifty-one years. That was how long ago he'd first met Santiago.

The old clockmaker had warned him that the time touch was dangerous. Elbert had disregarded this advice and had gone forth, searching.

He grabbed his walking stick and shuffled to his bookshelf. Smiling faces from rows of photographs looked back at him. They had been taken from his various journeys around the world, from the dunes of the Sahara to the valleys of northern Europe. He'd met people of all kinds. He'd met strangers who treated him like family, who welcomed him into their homes. He'd celebrated with them on joyful occasions. He'd delighted them with his old magic tricks. He had cried with them on rainy days, and comforted those hurt in the wars. To those, he vowed to one day rewind time to prevent their sadness.

To his surprise, many of them had refused.

"This treasure you seek," one of them had said, "is it worth giving up all you've gained on the journey to find it?"

As the adventures and memories piled on, the less eager Elbert became to reclaim the pendulum from the Barons, or to find the last piece of the time touch. In fact, a day came when he positively dreaded finding it.

Then, not long after, while exploring the shores of Spain with his group, he met a kind and thoughtful woman named Angie. Like him, Angie loved all things magic. But unlike him, she was not interested in changing history or gaining back lost time. She was interested in the future—their future together.

He abruptly quit his search for the key to the past.

At the center of the bookshelf was a photo of a man who looked like a younger version of Elbert. The man balanced a toddler on his leg. Elbert grinned as he touched the photo lightly.

There was a knock at the door. "Come in," he called.

The door swung open, bringing in a gust of wind and snow. On his doorstep were the two people from the photo. They both carried an armful of gift boxes.

"Merry Christmas, Father. Is Mother upstairs?"

"Yes. Just getting ready for the party."

The toddler ran forward and grabbed Elbert's leg. "Hi Grandpa! I saw a plane today!"

Elbert greeted his family. For the first time in a very long time, the ex-magician felt content.

CHAPTER TWENTY-FOUR

NEW YORK CITY, 2019

Ask anyone, and they'll likely agree Mondays are the worst days of the week, the dreaded day of going back to school or work after a long, restful weekend. Adam, however, could tolerate Mondays. After all, if Mondays didn't exist, there would be no looking forward to Fridays or the weekend.

The thirty-two-year-old stepped outside his office building during his lunch break. It was nice to give his eyes some downtime from his computer screen. His latest theorem required difficult calculations to prove, but he was certain he'd get there eventually. Mathematicians, after all, love a good challenge.

Rain splattered onto the streets of New York City. The trees had started to show their annual tinges of bright red and orange, and were decorating the sidewalks with the same. Adam thought about his lunch choices, and then headed for the nearest pretzel stand.

His cell phone rang. His wife, Rose, was calling to remind him to order cellophane wrappers for the Lugubrious Lollipops, and more cinnamon, too. Their joint bakery-and-confectionery shop was running low—all the pumpkin spice cookies had sold out within days. She also informed him they would have a special visitor that weekend.

"Good," answered Adam. "We have that new batch of cakes for Uncle Henry to test."

Uncle Henry made an appearance every now and then from the countryside where he'd retired, but each visit felt much too short. Adam and Rose were constantly testing new recipes, and the only person they could trust with the first taste test was Uncle Henry, who would always be honest—and, in Adam's view, the best baker around.

As he waited in line at the pretzel stand under the safety of his umbrella, he peeked into his briefcase. The snow globe rested inside, wrapped in delicate tissue paper. Adam gently laid a finger on the package. He carried the snow globe with him every day, wherever he went, in case the moment came. He had been waiting for twenty years. *It has to happen any day now.* So he told himself.

If there's one thing he learned from his youth, it's that time can't be rushed.

His patience paid off. And in fact, it happened on that very day. Past, present, and future looped together, tying themselves into a golden knot on that very sidewalk.

Someone accidentally jostled Adam as he stood in line. He did a double take as the person who had bumped him walked past. The dripping raincoat seemed awfully familiar.

Abruptly, Adam chased after the man. "Hey!"

The man turned and looked at Adam blankly. "Hello. May I help you?"

J.C. Walsh looked exactly the same as he had that first time he came into the Biscuit Basket twenty years ago. Adam stood still, at a loss for words. *It's him. It's really him.*

The older man lifted the sleeve of his raincoat to glance at his watch. "Er, if you don't mind," he said after some hesitation, "I have to get back to work."

Adam snapped back to his senses. With a flourish, he placed the package in the man's hand. "Listen carefully. There's a boy, a boy named Adam Lee Tripp, who needs your help."

"Excuse me?"

"His mouse, Speedy, is dying, and he's afraid of a lot of things. You will find him in a time where your present self isn't supposed to exist yet. He lives above a bakery—the Biscuit Basket, with velvet cakes and buttercream frosting. You'll tell him to go to the attic, where great, fantastic adventures await him." Adam nodded at the package. "And when you do, you'll be carrying a snow globe. This snow globe."

J.C. Walsh glanced around the street skeptically, as if checking to see whether this was a setup.

"Look, if this is some prank . . ." he began.

"Don't worry," Adam said with a reassuring smile. "This will make sense in due time. It will happen, because it has already happened. The boy is the one who will receive your music box—in which all is foretold."

"In which all is foretold," repeated J.C. Walsh with a confused look. The phrase sounded familiar, one he might have heard a long time ago.

The man scratched his gray-blond hair, a habit he'd acquired from his childhood due to constant itchiness from wearing his favorite aviator helmet. As he did, in the back of his mind, Jack saw his father sitting on the living room sofa, lighting the eleven striped candles on Jack's birthday cake, made with the family's special homemade buttercream frosting.

"Your grandfather always said candles are extraordinary things," Jack's father had commented. "Thousands of candles can be lit from a single candle, and the life of the first candle will not be shortened."

He then handed over a handsomely carved music box. "Happy eleventh birthday, Jack Charles Walsh," he'd told Jack. "This is a special gift passed down from your grandfather. He made a promise to a close friend to always keep this safe. He also made me promise to pass on this note he wrote."

There had been a small yellow card tucked in the crease of the lid. On it was written,

One in which all is foretold,
One in which lie gifts of gold,
One in which past days unfold.
Life goes round and round like a clock, dear Jack.
Enjoy it while you can.

"Grandpa Elbert always said only the second one can be controlled, and is worth pursuing," his father had said, chuckling. "Don't know what he meant by that. He was an odd fellow, always too cryptic for my taste. But a good man all the same. Take good care of this, you hear?"

Jack had kept the music box, right up to the day he had to leave his house behind.

After remembering all this, a look of stunned realization dawned on J.C. Walsh's face. He stared at Adam. "You're . . ." he whispered.

Adam smiled. "Good to see you too, friend."

ACKNOWLEDGMENTS

It takes a village to produce a book. None of this would have been possible without the following people.

A big thank-you to the wonderful team at Holiday House. An especially warm thank-you to my brilliant editor, Kelly Loughman, whose sharp eyes and attention to detail have improved this book tenfold. A thank-you to copyeditor Sue Wilkins, who caught inconsistencies the rest of us missed, and a thank-you to Gilbert Ford, for designing such an amazing cover.

Thank you, Adria Goetz, for taking a chance on an unknown author and for championing this book so enthusiastically.

A thank-you to the critique partners who helped improve this manuscript in its early stages, especially Mary and Christyne. I also want to thank my sister, Emily, for encouraging me after reading the very first draft. Thanks also to my mom and dad, who cheered me on in pursuing my dreams.

Last but not least, I want to thank my husband, Hayden, who supported me through ups and downs, who read multiple drafts, who calmed me down in times of anxiety. I am forever grateful to have you in my life.